ONE GOOD SHOT

Ken Ward

authorHOUSE®

AuthorHouse™ UK Ltd.
500 Avebury Boulevard
Central Milton Keynes, MK9 2BE
www.authorhouse.co.uk
Phone: 08001974150

©2010 Ken Ward. All rights reserved.

No part of this book may be reproduced, stored in a retrieval system, or transmitted by any means without the written permission of the author.

First published by AuthorHouse 8/27/2010

ISBN: 978-1-4520-7691-1 (sc)

k is printed on acid-free paper.

Acknowledgements

I would like to thank Caroline and all at Southgates Writing Group for all their support. Friends too numerous to mention for believing and encouraging.

Thank you to Ross Thomson and all the team at AuthorHouse for making everything run smoothly.

Thanks also to Rib, Marina and Jenny for their help with designing the cover.

Chapter One

Saturday September 10th 3.14pm

Joe Kipper had really enjoyed himself, since Lynn Rovers had given him a chance to carry on playing soccer. The knee injury that forced him to quit the professional game was holding up to non-league, which wasn't quite as pressurised. In three matches so far he had scored four goals and his obvious talent was shining through. Today's game was 15 minutes old, when the clearance from the keeper bounced past the defender and Joe was on it like a flash, a quick glance up and he saw it was him against their keeper. His only thought was one good shot is all it needs for goal number five. This was his last thought as he crumbled to the ground.

Two Years Earlier.

Four words could sum up Joes' life, he had it all beautiful house, well mansion would be a bet

All the flash cars and what could only be classed as a trophy wife. Alison was gorgeous a real cracker. Joe was good looking, with a physique men envied and women drooled over, he was six foot two, blonde and very athletic. He and Alison were like two pieces of a puzzle. Because of her looks though, the thing that people didn't realize at first was that she was very astute. In as much as Joe earned the money, she was the one who helped look after it, and it was really down to her that they did have something to show for it all. The main problem was that Joe liked to gamble. Alison knew this before they got married, but she had always been able to control his spending.

They had met three years ago in a casino, Joe was a regular visitor and Alison was a croupier on several of the roulette tables. These were a favourite with Joe. As Alison caught his eye he would spend his evenings at the casino, following her to whichever table she was working on. As they got to know each other he started to buy her drinks and then asked her out to dinner. This meant that Alison knew what Joe was like before she committed herself to him and their relationship.

Anyone on the outside looking in would find it hard to believe how quickly the good life could change. Most people who go to watch soccer would not have much sympathy with Joe's plight, believing it to be self-inflicted. All the money and the lifestyle that went with it could affect a person just as much as not having anything. You would wonder how it possible for someone with all that to be depressed, but this just what happened to Joe when suddenly everything d to disappear.

or the last four years he had been playing for Tallenbee

One Good Shot

United. He started with them as a teenager then he made it into the first team at twenty. Since then he had played in numerous cup finals and European competitions. Unfortunately all the success seemed to go to his head. Joe really enjoyed the gambling and also he had a collection of so called friends who were only too happy to help him spend his money. Alison worked hard to keep the spending in check.

Then one incident was to have a defining moment in Joe's life. It happened during the game that if they won, would mean they would win the league again. The tackle seemed to come from nowhere and it wasn't as bad as some had been. It hit him hard on the knee and was to prove to be one knock too many. The clubs medical staff did all they could, but despite all the rehabilitation, they just couldn't get the injury to heal enough to allow Joe to carry on playing. No one could say the club didn't do all they could, but after a year out it was decided that there was too much of a risk of long term injury, for Joe to carry on playing at the level he was used to. This was when the problems really started because even though he wasn't playing; Joe kept spending money as if he was still earning. The club had slowly reduced what they were paying him and eventually it was agreed to let him go with compensation. Alison knew this money wouldn't last long and she made it clear to Joe that she would stay and support him but that he really needed to cut back on what was being spent. These helped Joe because one of his fears was that Alison would get fed up and want to leave, so even though Joe didn't like the idea very much he knew it had to happen. He also realised that Alison was the reason he had managed to keep his sanity over the last year.

As word spread about his injury and his gambling, the agents who used to ring all the time to offer positions with other teams, stopped contacting him, and when he spoke to them there always seemed an excuse why they couldn't help him. It soon became obvious to Joe, that apart from Alison he was on his own, and if he wanted to stay in soccer he would have to look to a lower league. It was Alison who suggested that they sell the house and use the money to buy somewhere smaller and more sensible. Alison also thought it possible that Joe could find a local and smaller club to play for. Even though this had occurred to Joe, it didn't make it any easier for him to deal with. Alison knew that Joe still gambled she just didn't realise the amount of debt he was in. The one good point in all this for Joe was it meant he could get away from his bookie Ted Bloom, if only for a short time.

One Year Earlier

This was how they ended up in Norfolk; Joe had to admit the area seemed nice. He had been to see the local team Lynn Rovers a couple of times since they had moved. Alison was happier as some of her family lived in the area and so she settled in really quickly. Lynn Rovers appeared to Joe to be a good outfit for a non-league team. The important question was, would they take a chance on him? Once he met with the clubs owners and talked things over they seemed prepared to take that chance. They knew all about his injury from the media coverage at the time. Through the media they also knew about his gambling and the problems this had caused, Joe assured them that it was all in the past. After several hours talk it was agreed that Joe would play for them on a pay as you play contract because of his knee. Joe explained that he felt the slightly slower pace of the game would enable his knee to deal with it. Part of his contract was that if his injury was to flare up again and he wasn't able to play for a lengthy period of time, the club could release him without compensation. Unknown to the club Joe wouldn't play many games for them, there again Joe didn't know this either.

The moment Joe had thought about but had been dreading happened one day after training. Two burly characters approached him as he made his way across to his car. They pulled him to one side and the tallest one said, 'Mr Bloom would like a word.' Ted Bloom was the last person Joe wanted to see, as he knew he would be after some of the money he owed him. The two guys made it clear that the matter wasn't up for discussion as they took hold of Joe by his arms and bundled him into the back of their car. After driving for about thirty minutes they pulled over onto a dirt track and Joe saw Ted's jaguar parked at the side. One of the henchmen told Joe to go and get in the jag, Joe moved very carefully out of the car and across to the other, he didn't fancy upsetting either of these two. It was as if he was being greeted by an old friend as Ted said,

'How are you Joe, lovely to see you again?'

'Alright Ted.'

Joe was very apprehensive about how this meeting was going to go. When he last thought about how much money he owed Ted he guessed it was about £20,000, and with the situation he was in now, he really didn't see how he could pay it off. After some more small talk, mainly from Ted, Joe turned to him and said,

'Come on then let's get down to the point of this.'

There was no way Joe was prepared for the answer he got. Ted told him that there was a way his debt could be wiped out and he would only have to do a small favour. The problem was it was something that Joe would never have dreamed of doing, he would have to arrange to fix some matches through the season. Ted explained that even though it was only non-league football, betting was substantial especially in the local area. A group of foreign businessmen were looking to make some money out of it. Joe had always heard gossip that this sort of thing went on in a lot of sports, but he had never been put in this position before. All they were asking was that Joe waited and he would be contacted and told what they wanted the result to be. Joe couldn't believe what he was hearing and looked at Ted saying,

'You'll get your money but not like this and you can tell whoever is behind it to Fuck Off!'

Ted smirked and replied,

'Think about it and someone will be in touch.'

'I don't need to think about.' said Joe as he opened the car door.

He was grabbed by the arms and thrown on the side of the track and as he looked up both cars sped off. Joe pulled himself up and wandered home, his head was spinning. His first thought was I could get rid of all my debts, but what about my new teammates. As he carried on walking he decided there was no way he was going to do it, his next aim was to make sure Alison didn't find out what had happened.

A week later a letter arrived for Joe at the football club it simply told him that the game at the weekend had to be lost; he would then hear more when needed. Match day arrived and Joe was literally running himself ragged, he was doing everything he could to make sure that Lynn Rovers won the game. Joe scored once and Lynn won 2—1. Joe was very wary as he made his way across to his car, there was no-one waiting to accost him so he decided that he had called their bluff, and as far as he was concerned he had got the better of them. How wrong he was. On the Monday when he returned to his car after training, an envelope had been left on his windscreen. He tore the letter open and unfolded the piece of paper on which the words That was very foolish and you will regret it!! Were scrawled. Joe balled the note up and threw it away, vowing not to think about it anymore. As Joe ran out for the next game he had started to forget about the threat, as he had heard no more from anyone.

Saturday September 10th 3.15pm

As Joe was thinking one good shot, Jack French stood above the pitch looking down with exactly the same thought; all I need is one good shot. There was a quiet pop as the silenced rifle released its fury. The bullet hit Joe just as he was about to strike the ball. No one on the pitch or around it could believe what had happened as Joe crumbled to the ground, had his knee gone again. The first aid team raced on and the look of shock on their faces was horrific, as they moved Joe and saw the bullet hole in his shirt. It was clear Joe had died instantly as the bullet hole was directly over his heart. One of the medics screamed at the ref to get everyone off the pitch as quickly as possible, and for someone to call the police and ambulance. The medical team got Joe off the pitch as soon as they could. They didn't let anyone know what they had found; this would wait for the police to organize things. The few police at the ground along with the stewards were making arrangements for the supporters to stay where they were. P.C. Tim Jarvis, who was at the ground, put a call through to the station for someone to contact D.I. Ray Keane and get him to the soccer ground as soon as possible.

Chapter Two

Jack French had his rifle packed up and was making his way from the area before all the fuss started down below him. This hit had been one of the easier ones he had done. He worked on the theory that things went smoothly because of the planning he put in. He was relatively sure that no one had taken any notice of him the previous week. He had come along to check out the site and the view he would have, with his camera in hand snapping away he mingled in with the other visitors to the park. Even when he took pictures overlooking the football pitch, he felt safe in the knowledge that he wasn't standing out at all. He had first heard two weeks ago that his services might be needed if Joe Kipper didn't go along with what was suggested to him. Jack had come along to the site to choose his point from where he would complete the job. The place he chose had a perfect view of the soccer pitch. He was on a raised area of the park, which would make his shot easier. His only concern was the houses behind him, but when he turned round it appeared that the trees would shield him from prying eyes. As always he was sure that any description given of him would match any number of people in the area at the time. This was all part of the planning in that he would dress to blend in with others around. He decided he would wear jeans and a t-shirt, and a hat to help shield his eyes. The only thing special he would have on was a pair of trainers that had no pattern on the soles so he would leave very little in the way of footprints. Jack left satisfied that he could make the hit and his getaway as soon as he was given the go ahead.

The call came the following Wednesday, he was told to do the job as soon as possible. Jack's reply was

'Okay I will deal with it, make sure the money is ready to be deposited.' 'It will be.' Then the caller rang off.

He decided the following Saturday would do. On that morning Jack arrived in Lynn early and made his way into the town. He looked just like any other shopper with his holdall but unknown to anyone else the contents were very different to shopping. In his bag he had his favourite rifle along with its silencer. This meant all you would hear would be a slight popping noise as he fired. Jack was so sure of himself that he always worked on the theory that one shot was all he needed. He made his way to the park and the adrenalin started pumping. This was good as long as it was under control.

Saturday September 10th 3.20pm

As Jack made his way from the scene, down on the pitch there was chaos. There was shock, and then horror at what had just happened. The clubs security team were organizing things as best they could. There was an announcement over the P.A. system asking people to stay where they were, until the stewards and the few police there got the situation under control. The police who had been called arrived very quickly. D.S. Jenny Woods, as the most senior officer in attendance made it her first job to get an announcement out that the

One Good Shot

match had been abandoned. You could hear a collective moan of grief when it was followed by the news that Joe had been shot. The first problem for the police was that they had about a thousand witnesses, yet in reality no one had seen anything. Jenny decided the easiest way to deal with everyone was to ask anyone with any information to contact a police officer otherwise people could leave the ground.

For Alison the day was to end in a dreadful way. In one respect it would turn out to be a relief that she wasn't at the game and she had been visiting relatives. She had no idea what to expect when the police car parked outside the house in the early evening. Fortunately the W.P.C. was quick and caught Alison as she fainted, when they broke the news of what had happened. The police told Alison it was going to be a while before they would be able to fully explain the situation. W.P.C. Sue Harbour had dealt with several grieving relatives in her time in the force. She made Alison a mug of sweet tea, then sat with her and explained,

'All we really know at the moment is that Joe was shot in the chest, and as far as I know he died immediately. We will need to do a post mortem with your permission.'

'Of course do what you need to do.' Alison sobbed.

'They have searched the surrounding area but not found anything to help much.' Alison nodded as way of reply.

'D.I. Ray Keane will be in charge of the case and he will want to talk to you soon.'

Then Sue suggested that as they expected a surge of media interest because of Joe's past exploits, it might be a good idea if Alison could stay somewhere else for the time being. Alison was finding it difficult to take in all that the Sue was saying. It sounded as though her voice was coming from down a tunnel and it was if she was in a different room. Her immediate thoughts after being given the news were I will never hold Joe again. Also a feeling of helplessness as to whether this was in some way her fault. If she hadn't pushed Joe to move he might still be alive. When she voiced this opinion to Sue, she replied,

'There will be all different feelings and emotions running wild for the next few weeks, possibly months. All I can say is you have to try and view things in reality. From previous experience you will then know what is important. Just keep reminding yourself what you had with Joe and that his death is not to do with you.'

For a moment this helped Alison, and then the tears started to flow again as though someone had turned tap on. Sue put her arm around her and just held her while she sobbed. In her short career Sue had dealt with many grieving relatives and knew that it helped just to have someone there.

Chapter Three

Alison rang her parents and between sobs of anguish, explained what had happened to Joe. When she told them about staying somewhere else her dad told her he was on his way to pick her up. The W.P.C. was left to stay with her and took down the details of her parents address to pass on to D.I. Keane, for when he needed to speak to her.

D.I. Ray Keane could be a bit gruff in how he dealt with people, but this was put down to him having been in the police for near to 25 years and some of the people he had to deal with. Even though the other officers only mentioned it behind his back he knew their nickname for him was mustard. He took this as a compliment on his success and the fact he would never give up on a case till he got the result he felt it deserved.

Ray had been brought up to date on what had happened in a phone call that afternoon, and immediately made his way to the football ground. During his career he had seen many deaths but first reports of what had happened made this one seem weird. There weren't too many deaths by shooting in the area, so Rays' first impression was it had something to do with Joe Kippers' past. Most reports of gunshots in the region were as a result of a holidaymaker or a newcomer being shocked to hear gun fire then amazed when they were told it was only a farmer or other local, partaking in some sport. It never ceased to surprise Ray that people from large towns or cities still only associated gun shots with crime. This was one of the humorous sides of the job, only equalled by some officers being asked by holidaying people if anything could be done about the noise of seagulls. Then some people would be upset when the officer would try and explain that the call of the birds was part of being near the sea, and they should just enjoy the sounds of the wildlife. Ray had read all the gossip in the local press on what Joes' life had been like before he came to Lynn. When he reached the soccer ground, the place seemed to be a mass of confusion. As he made his way towards the melee of police officers he could sense the organisation, and as usual his officers seemed to have things under control.

'Afternoon sir.' was the first response from P.C. Tim Jarvis who Ray knew was a very enthusiastic young officer, he could be a bit over enthusiastic at times but he got on with the job and worked hard.

'Why has the body been moved? What is going on here?'

'All I can say Sir is that human nature overruled common sense and the medical team got the body off the scene immediately. In their defence I would say that once they saw he had been shot they were panicking, and were just aware of clearing everyone away as quickly as they could.'

'Okay I don't suppose it would have helped any seeing where the body dropped. Just make sure that area is cordoned off for now. Then bring me up to speed then Tim.'

'It is still a bit unclear sir. All I can tell you at the

moment is that Joe Kipper has been shot and killed. We are searching the park up above the ground, but as yet nothing of any help has turned up.'

'Call the team from the mortuary. I want the body taken to the hospital as discreetly as possible; we don't want the local news photographer to have pictures of the body being removed. If necessary get the team to drive in from the far end away from the main road and entrance.'

The activity on the pitch had quietened down as the body had been removed. People were slowly making their way away. The majority were in shock; so far the police hadn't found anyone who could help as no one had been looking up from the game. The hope for the police would be that someone in the park, or the houses overlooking the ground, might have seen something. Ray decided he could leave the officers at the ground to deal with things, and he made his way to the park to see what was happening. The local press were already about and Ray knew it wouldn't be long before word got out to the nationals, especially considering Joe's past. A reporter cornered him as he made his way through the park and asked,

'Do you know what's happening yet?'

'Give us a chance,' replied Ray "There will be a statement as soon as possible."

Once Ray got up to above the stadium he started off by looking around between the trees to see what a sniper would have seen down on the pitch from in amongst the trees. Ray could work out that for a professional, which this had obviously been; it was an ideal situation with a good view of the pitch. At the same time however you would be quite well hidden from the houses that followed the path around the park. The initial response to the house to house didn't seem to hold out much hope for the police. No one had seen anything that appeared suspicious or heard anything unusual. There had been a lot of people out in the park enjoying the sunshine. Ray decided to leave D.S. Jenny Woods in charge of the officers in the park and said to her,

'I'm going to see the wife now and see if she can throw any light on the matter.'

'Okay sir I'll see you later at the station.'

After Ray had been to see Alison, he would issue a statement to the press.

He would inform them that Joe Kipper had died from a single gunshot, and that his officers would do all they could to find the killer as quickly as possible. Ray knew that a media scrum would ensue once the story broke.

The one thing that Ray was happy with was that D.S.Jenny Woods had been the first senior officer on the scene. He knew she was a very good officer but also they had had a relationship of sorts for some time. It had happened slowly after she had been there for support when his wife had died. So far they had been able to keep the relationship under wraps which they both realised they had to do. It was frowned upon by the powers that be for officers who worked together to have any sort of dealings apart from work ones. Ray was ten years older than Jenny but she was not bothered by this. As she always said when he brought the subject up age is only a number. Even though it meant they had to be secretive around the others, Ray found it a help when they were working a case to be able to discuss things in a formal atmosphere, then when the opportunity arose they could talk it through in a more relaxed way. This suited Ray

One Good Shot

and he felt it helped their relationship. When they first got together Ray had suggested one of them could put in for a transfer, but Jenny had made him see that as they both liked the area, they should wait and see how things went. That had been three years ago now and still they were sure no-one was aware of their feelings. Also whenever Ray got concerned about things coming out, Jenny always made him laugh by pointing out that he would soon be up for retirement and well before her so it wouldn't be a problem anymore. As was usual in situations like theirs where they didn't think anyone was aware of things, others had picked up on signs. The first person to have noticed was Lisa Hall the forensics officer, but fortunately for them both she was discreet and felt that if it didn't affect their work then it was no-one else's business. Over time a few others had seen that there was more than just a work relationship developing, after some initial friendly banter it had been forgotten and Ray was quite sure they could carry on as they were, without any problems.

Chapter Four

Ray made his way to see Alison at her parents' house. As he drove, he was trying to piece things together in his mind, as to what had happened earlier that afternoon. It was difficult to grasp that Joe Kipper had been shot in full view of everyone. Already Ray was thinking it had to have something to do with his past. He couldn't see that Joe had been in the area long enough to upset anyone locally so badly. He made up his mind that once he had spoken to the wife, he would need to contact the police in Tallenbee, to see if they knew anything that might help. Ray had to admit to himself when he saw Alison Kipper she was certainly a good looking woman, she fitted the bill for a footballer's wife. He took her to be 5'5" tall, blonde with beautiful blue eyes, at the present time the blue eyes were fighting a losing battle against puffiness and redness, and it looked as though she had been crying constantly since the news had been broken to her. He introduced himself and expressed his sympathy,

'I hope you will understand that even though it is very difficult, I do need to ask you some questions.'

'That's okay,' replied Alison, "But I don't know what I can tell you. I have tried thinking of why this has happened.

I have even talked it over with the other officer; it just does not seem to make any sense."

'Firstly it is really to see if you can think of any reason why this may have happened, I hear what you are saying about already going over things. Just sometimes it needs to be talked about more than once, and you would be amazed how that can jog the memory. Such as do you know who Joe has been involved with, or anyone he may have upset?'

'When you say involved with you are not suggesting he has another woman are you?'

'No not at all, though if you don't mind me saying so that must have been something you had to deal with in the past. Women who would try their luck with a good looking sportsman are nothing new. I was thinking more along the lines of people he may have upset who would look for revenge in such away.'

Alison explained that it was no secret about Joe's gambling in the past, but as far as she knew that had all been sorted out when they had moved to Lynn.

'Okay,' said Ray "I'm sure you realise I will need to talk to you again soon, but I will leave you now. Just let the officer know if there is anything you need."

'Thank you, all I can think of at the moment is it would help if you could keep the press away.'

'I will do my best,' replied Ray as he made his way outside.

Ray felt bad at how he had made Alison feel with his questions but he knew you always started an investigation like he was about to undertake by looking at the family life. And in the case of a known star it was possible that there could be many enemies. Having now met Alison he was more than ever convinced this was connected to Joes' past and in particular the gambling. He would keep an open mind and would change his judgement if necessary, after he had spoke with the team and once he met Alison again in a few days time.

Ray left Alison and made his way back to the station, his team were in the process of setting up an incident room. Several officers were starting to make their way through witness statements that had been taken at the soccer ground. As had been realised earlier, they had not really got a decent statement from any of them, for nearly 1,000 people at the stadium none of them had been looking up from the action on the pitch. Even though it was now early evening Ray decided he needed to set wheels in motion for finding out about Joe's past, he phoned the local police in Tallenbee. Ray had heard all about the gambling but even he was taken back when they told him that Joe owed a local bookmaker Ted Bloom close to £20,000, and that this figure could be higher as Joe's name had come up in a previous investigation into the bookies, as Ted Bloom was known to be a shady character.

The officer he spoke to told Ray he would leave a message for D.I. Robert Simmons to ring him the next day so they could discuss things further.

Robert Simmons rang the following morning and he agreed with Ray's suggestion to him of putting some men onto doing background checks in the area, and he told Ray they would liaise with his team to be of any help they could be. Ray thanked him and explained that he felt they were going to need all the help they could get; in particular this was an unusual crime for them to be dealing with. The next

One Good Shot

thing that needed Ray's attention was the post mortem; this had been arranged to take place as soon as the body had been taken to the local hospital. It was going to be done immediately mainly because of the unusual nature of the killing for the area. All Ray felt he needed to know first was what sort of weapon he was looking for; obviously the post mortem would also look to find out if Joe had been taking any substances. It was straight forward that he had died from the gunshot.

The post mortem took place in the early evening, it was agreed that Joe had died from a gunshot from a powerful rifle. The bullet had entered his chest and lodged in his heart, the doctor confirmed the findings of the medics at the soccer ground that Joe was dead before he hit the ground. The bullet was removed and Ray bagged it to send off to ballistics for them to run their tests to let him know exactly what the weapon had been. The toxicology tests were completed and were all negative, Joe's body was in as good a shape as expected for an athlete. The police saw no reason now that the body couldn't be released to the family for burial, as there was no suspicion surrounding Joe as far as the death was concerned it was not felt that the body would reveal anything else to help the police. Ray left the hospital and went to the soccer ground to check how things were progressing. After this he made his way to the police station to clear things up for the night. The only new lead to come to light was a phone call from a man who lived in one of the houses near the ground; he had told the officer he had seen a person amongst the trees above the pitch. Ray rang him back and told him he would visit him first thing on the Sunday morning to talk in more detail about what he had seen and maybe he would like to write something down while things were fresh in his mind. Ray was used to not working normal office hours on any case but he also knew the need for himself and his team to get proper rest. The evening shift would work through the paperwork gathered so far and then Sunday morning the team would start moving things forward.

On the Sunday morning the soccer ground had opened the gates for shocked fans to pay their respects to Joe. He may not have been with the team very long but he had made a good impression. A lot of local fans had been amazed when it had been revealed that Joe Kipper was to sign for their team, some of them had followed his career as a striker with Tallenbee United as that was the closest local team in footballs top tier. By lunchtime there had been more people through the gates than usually came to games. The penalty area where Joe had slumped so dramatically to the ground less than twenty four hours earlier was buried underneath a carpet of flowers.

Ray visited the ground in the afternoon, to see for himself what the reaction had been. Also he needed to discuss things with the owners as to what would happen next. As a mark of respect the game planned for Wednesday evening had been postponed and as the team's next home game wasn't for two weeks, it was decided that there should not be any reason why it could not take place.

Chapter Five

On the Sunday morning Ray had had a meeting with his chief, Superintendent Adam Church to bring him up to date with the case. He agreed with Ray that the shooting had something to do with Joe's past he expressed his opinion to Ray that they could do with wrapping the case up as soon as possible. This would help calm the local people down and to show that even though they were a small force they could deal with things efficiently. Ray also knew that Adam liked things to be nice and neat even when it was obvious that things would take time. He always had the feeling that Adam had forgotten what being an officer in the frontline was like. If ever someone was well suited to being a pen pusher it was him.

'Make sure that we work together with the other force on this one Ray.'

'Okay sir, we will make as much progress as quickly as we can, I don't think the locals have a lot to fear though.'

Ray made his way to see Terry Jennings who had rang the night before. He looked in on Jenny his D.S and said,

'Chase up the guys in Tallenbee for me, and find out what they have turned up.'

'Okay sir, I'll let you know what they say when you get back.'

Ray gave her a quick smile that no-one else would take any notice of, but for them it meant a lot.

'Come in.' Terry Jennings said when he answered the door to Ray, "I'll just put the kettle on then we can talk."

'Thanks very much, I'll have coffee please Sir.'

Once they had their drinks, Terry took Ray outside and showed him where he had seen the person yesterday in the trees. He told Ray it wasn't unusual to see people in the park in the nice weather, but this person caught Terry's eye because he was standing in amongst the trees very still,

'I saw him standing right over there, but I went back indoors for a minute and when I came back out he had gone.'

Terry explained that he had thought no more of it until he heard that the police had been knocking on doors last night asking if anyone had seen anything unusual during the afternoon. He explained he had gone out through the afternoon. When he heard about the shooting and that the police had been round, he felt that he had to ring. He had given a description as best as he could to the officer, but the person had been very nondescript. This actually described Jack French who always made a point of not attracting attention. Ray went and had another look around in the trees where Terry had pointed to, there was nothing obvious but Ray decided to call forensics back for another detailed search now they had an area to concentrate on. While Ray was waiting he wandered carefully around amongst the trees, he could see the appeal to a sniper which was how Ray pictured this person to be as it was becoming increasingly more certain that this had been a professional killing. Ray looked behind him and could see that even though Terry had seen the person from his garden it wouldn't be difficult for the killer to move slightly and then be out of sight, the trees would have shielded him from view. In the opposite direction there was a good view down to the soccer pitch, this case was leaving Ray with a lot of mixed thoughts, he was sure it was to do with Joe's past but it was proving just as hard to find out what the connection was. The gambling had to have something to do with it he thought, so they needed to find out where Joe did his gambling and how Ted Bloom was involved.

As Ray came back out from the trees he saw Lisa Hall from the forensic team pull up in her van.

'Hi Lisa.'

'Hello Ray, have you been messing up my crime scene.'

'No I have been careful, all I can tell you is a gentleman in the houses over there says he saw someone in those trees yesterday.'

'You don't sound convinced.'

'No, I think he saw someone, but he might think it is important because of our questions.'

'Leave it with me and I'll see if I can turn up anything useful for you, I'll let you have my report as soon as possible.'

'Thanks Lisa I'll speak to you later.'

Ray made his way back to the police station after telling Terry they would be in touch if they needed any more information. As he walked back into the station Jenny called after him, just for a moment they were alone in the corridor and very briefly there was a touch of hands.

'I may have some news to cheer you up Sir.'

'I really hope so Jenny.'

It took Jenny about 20 minutes to bring Ray up to date with what she had found out from the police in Tallenbee. Ray left Jenny to go to his office feeling much better about things. He needed to speak to D.I. Robert Simmons himself, but Jenny had given him all the known details about Joe's gambling, and that also there had been problems with a bookie in the past. This meant it looked as though it would be as good a place as any to start. After Ray had spoken to Robert he decided that he needed to speak with Joe's wife Alison again, because he had a niggling feeling that she must have known something about the bookmaker Ted Bloom. Now at least they had a name connected with Joe's past to give them something to work on.

Sunday evenings were always a good time of the week for Ray. This was when he and Jenny would drive out of town and find a quiet restaurant where they would not be known. Ray was always feeling that he wasn't being fair to Jenny in their relationship. She would always tell him not to be worried as she knew what she had got into, once they realised their feelings for each other. Once they had ordered Ray smiled and then said,

'You know that this case is going to take up a lot of time now don't you?'

'I know but we will still be talking to each other, even if only at work.'

'Yes I know that. There is a chance I'm going to have to go to Tallenbee to continue part of the investigation. I don't

One Good Shot

think it is a good idea that I suggest you come with me, we don't need tongues wagging do we?'

'Of course not. You know how I feel about you Ray, and I don't intend doing anything to ruin that. Just an idea though if you have to take someone with you what about Tim, he seems keen and he is a good lad.'

'Yes I agree. I will try and ring you in the evenings when I'm free.'

'I know you will, but as you always say let's concentrate on the matter in hand first.'

They had a very enjoyable meal and the evening ended too quickly for either of them. They left both looking forward to their next chance to meet up.

Chapter Six

Ray decided that as it was now dragging into Sunday evening, he would go and see Jenny and tell her that they should see about getting off home. As far as anyone in the room was aware it was just the boss letting Jenny know what was happening, no-one appeared to take any notice of the glance between them. They were the only ones aware that they would meet for a meal later. She could start making enquiries about the bookie first thing on the Monday morning, while he would go and see Alison Kipper. They arranged to meet at lunchtime and see where they were up to. Ray was also hopeful that by then they might have the forensic report from Lisa Hall.

The following morning, Ray went straight to Alison's parent's home. When he arrived he was pleased to see so far the press hadn't been able to find out where Alison was staying and so no-one was pestering her. Alison looked a lot fresher than when Ray had last seen her, she was visibly relieved when Ray told her that Joe's body had been released for burial. Ray did suggest that she might want to wait a short while before arranging the funeral as this might give some of the press other stories to follow. The hope would be that by waiting the funeral would not turn into a media circus, Ray knew the funeral would be big because of Joe's past but he just wanted to make things as easy as possible for Alison. Once Alison's mum had settled Ray down with coffee and biscuits he got down to the reason he was there for.

'Firstly Alison does the name Ted Bloom mean anything to you at all.'

Ray noticed the sharp intake of breath from Alison before she gathered herself to reply,

'Yes it does, but I thought that was all in the past.'

'Sorry I don't think so, according to the officers in Tallenbee, Ray owes him in excess of £20,000.'

Again Ray couldn't help noticing that this had shaken Alison.

'I thought Joe had sorted all that out before we moved.'

Ray sat talking things through with Alison but basically it appeared she didn't know anything much about Joe's dealing with Ted, apart from trying to get him to stop gambling. She had always tried to control Joe's spending, but he always seemed to have money to spend on gambling.

'As far as trying to stop Joe gambling it was a bit like King Canute trying to stop the sea, also when Joe was earning top money the bookies were only too willing to give him credit.'

Ray left Alison promising her he would do all he could to catch the person who had killed Joe, he also told her that he thought it went deeper than a disgruntled bookmaker. Ray made his way back to Lynn police station with thoughts racing through his mind as to what could have happened to get Joe killed.

When he got back he went to his office and was pleased to see that on his desk was the forensic report from Lisa. Unfortunately the report didn't throw any light on the matter in hand. The only thing that Lisa could tell them was that there had been some flattening of the undergrowth, in amongst the trees this was consistent with someone trampling about in the trees. There had been no definite footprints though the ground looked scuffed; it stood out because you wouldn't expect much activity in that area. Lisa concluded in her report that she and her team had checked all the area but had found no evidence of any use to them; they had gathered some pieces of what could only be described as rubbish, this had been bagged up with the hope that something else picked up later in the investigation would be tied in with it. Really this was more in hope for a lucky break as so often happened in police work. This led her to believe that they were dealing with a professional as it was harder now to not leave any forensics behind.

The disappointment made Ray's mind up, that he would go and see Jenny to see what they had found about the bookie, and also chase his team up a little. He explained that they needed to really dig around to help solve this case. The next thing would be to arrange to travel to Tallenbee and meet with the local police and set up an interview with Ted Bloom. He made his way to the incident room and on the way he met Jenny who was on her way to the canteen for some lunch, when Ray heard where she was headed he said

'I think I'll join you for a bite.'

Over lunch Jenny told him that from her chat with Tallenbee station it appeared that Ted Bloom was well known locally as being an unsavoury character with a reputation for

One Good Shot

allowing people credit, but not adverse to using threatening tactics to get his money back. Ray left Jenny in the canteen and made his way to see Superintendent Adam Church to bring him up to date, and arrange with him for the journey to Tallenbee. Adam agreed it might well help for Ray to go and see Ted Bloom, he was also happy for Tim Jarvis to go as well, it was a big part of Adam's regime to encourage young officers. Ray left to see Tim and tell him to go home and pack some clothes and to be back at the station in an hour. Whilst he waited, the opportunity to go and see Jenny once more was not to be passed up. It was easy enough to cover the real reason for seeing her by telling her to chase up ballistics for the test results on the bullet while he was in Tallenbee. Ray was ready to go when Tim returned as he always had an overnight case in the boot of his car through experience of things happening without warning. At 4o'clock on the Monday, Ray and Tim left for Tallenbee with Ray hoping they were on the way to getting some answers.

Chapter Seven

Whenever Ray had to drive out of Lynn he always understood what people meant about the roads around the area, even early in the week, evening traffic was terrible. He also realised just what a nightmare the traffic lads must have as he took notice of some diabolical driving, being done by people who obviously just had one thing in mind, to get home. He could tell by watching that these people obviously drove the same route each day, and there was no allowance made for anything being different around them. He was aware that there was no rush to get to Tallenbee, according to his satellite navigation it would take about three hours to get there. A hotel had been arranged for them both to stay at and meeting planned with D.I.Robert Simmons on the Tuesday morning at nine. Ray spent the journey discussing the case with Tim and he found it interesting to see the enthusiasm that Tim displayed, even though they hadn't really got anywhere yet. The time also gave Ray a chance outside of work to talk to Tim and hear about his hopes for the future. Ray found it refreshing to hear someone speak about their hopes for their career unlike some of the older guys who would always tell you that the job wasn't like the old days. Ray knew this for himself but he was also glad to encourage youth as they were more adept at changing with the demands the work made on them. It was interesting to listen to Tim as well because a lot of young officers were second or third generation policeman, but Tim explained he was the first one of his family to join the force and it had just appealed to him. Ray smiled to himself, at the same time as hoping that enthusiasm would stay in place, he felt it was possible as long as Tim received the correct help and saw positive results. He knew this case could be a big help in that direction. The traffic started to ease off and Ray found that even though the case was still on his mind for the first time since Saturday afternoon he started to relax a little bit. Just after 7o'clock Tim pointed out the hotel in the centre of Tallenbee, Ray pulled into the car park and they went to check in. They met up at 8o'clock in the dining room and while they ate dinner Ray pushed Tim to give him more of his thoughts on the case so far. Tim found that he was enjoying being asked for his ideas. This was the first time since he had joined that a senior officer was asking him his opinion. He had heard a lot about Ray when he was first posted to Lynn. But he had learnt even while still studying that you took what others said about someone with a pinch of salt, as his mum used to remind of. It was always better to make your own mind up about people. Tim was also quick to know when taking notice of someone could also be a help to himself. He was thoughtful before he answered with his ideas.

'My first reaction on hearing the possibility that the bookie was involved in Joes' death was that it was like something out of a film. But as we heard more about Joes' gambling it seemed a more logical reason.'

Ken Ward

Ray agreed,

'So we can only wait till the morning then, and see what Mr Bloom has to say for himself.'

On the Tuesday morning Ray had his breakfast early, this was something that had become routine since he had been on his own. He was always awake well before necessary but he decided that sometimes it was the best part of the day. Quite often he would be out walking by the river just to watch the sun breaking through the early cloud. To a lot of people who lived in the area the early morning calling of the seagulls that followed the few remaining fishing boats into harbour, were nothing short of a nuisance, to Ray they were a sign of life and the start of a new day. Five years ago with the death of his wife it was this that helped pull him back from the brink of depression as simple as it was; he knew how easy it would have been too slowly give up. His memory of his dad was that you could find the answer in a drink, Ray felt fortunate that he didn't agree and with his work and now the time spent with Jenny he knew he had been right. Then he rang Jenny to see if she had heard anything from ballistics, and when she told him no, he told her to chase them up straight away. Even though Ray knew that the tests could take some time to complete, as usual like all officers he felt his enquiry should take priority over all others. Ray finished the call by being able to tell Jenny that he was missing her already and couldn't wait to be able to see her again. Jenny replied that she missed him too, she had to bit more discreet than Ray as she was in the incident room and others could be listening.

Ray and Tim then made their way to the local police station to meet D.I. Robert Simmons, Tim was taken back when he went inside, and the station was a lot larger than Lynn but it was also very modern he was impressed. D.I. Simmons was in his office when the desk sergeant showed them in.

'Good morning gentlemen, nice to meet you.'

'And you.' Replied Ray

'Nice office Sir.' Said Tim

'Yes it is very nice; mind you a comfy office doesn't make the job any easier, especially with characters like Ted Bloom around.' Ray looked around and thought that even though the station and the office were very nice it was just like many other office buildings in the area. Though it made no difference to results the station in Lynn had appeal and character. It was an old building that looked out on the parks in the town and Ray had always liked the view approaching the building and also the view you could get across the town from the upstairs rooms. Sometimes when relaxing with some of the others it was joked that Ray and the old building suited one another. To a point he agreed mainly because since he had taken the position at Lynn which was like coming home for Ray he had felt comfortable. His family had lived in one of the little villages just outside the hustle of the town for several generations. Like Tim he was the first policeman in the family. His father till his death and now his brothers all worked on the family farm. His brother Mike had always said Ray joined the police because he knew what hard work the farm was. Ray had helped out on the farm when he was growing up; the thing that had led to him joining the police was after an officer had come to the school when Ray was fifteen. After listening to the officer and his enthusiasm for the job Ray decided that was what he wanted to do, and his family had been very supportive of his choice. He had worked hard for the rest of his schooling and got the grades to go to training school and had never looked back. Despite the joking he was also aware that they were very proud of him. They just never let on to him.

He brought himself back to the real reason they were here for. And asked what the officers had managed to get from Ted Bloom, when they had spoken to him.

'Not a lot really, I do feel he might just be a small cog in a larger wheel. They did say that he seemed very sure of himself. He had been quite happy when they had asked him to come to the station.

It had been arranged for Ted Bloom to be at the police station at 10o'clock and Ray and Tim would have a chat with him. Rays' first impression of Ted was similar to the others that he was very sure of himself. Ray took note of how he was conducting himself. He was smartly dressed and sat behind the desk with a distinct smirk on his face that suggested he thought that he had the beating of a couple of coppers from a small town station.

'Good morning Mr Bloom, I'm D.I. Ray Keane and this is P.C. Tim Jarvis, we are from Lynn and would like to talk to you about Joe Kipper.'

'Talk away mate, all I know is he owed me money and now I'm being told he is dead. And your lot just want to keep me from my work by asking silly questions.'

'When did you last see Joe then?'

'Ages ago, he just disappeared then I heard about him being killed when you lot came to see me.'

'So you didn't try to chase him up for your money then.'

'How could I when I didn't know where he was.'

'I wouldn't have thought it would be too difficult for

someone like you to track someone down. In particular when they owed you such a large sum of money.'

'In my line of business you win some, you lose some.'

'So are you telling me that when Joe disappeared, you were prepared to just write off his debt?'

'Something like that yeah, I would make up the money from other punters wouldn't I.'

Ray looked at Ted and decided that they weren't going to get any more from him for now, so told him that they were finished talking to him for now, but they would definitely want to talk to him again before they returned to Lynn. Also he was informed that other officers would stay in contact with him after that. With a cocky note in his voice Ted looked up and said,

'I hope they won't be around too long, it isn't good for business for people to see the police hanging around all the time.'

'It might surprise you to hear that I'm not really bothered about your business, I'm investigating a murder and I can promise you I will keep on looking until I find out what happened and who killed Joe Kipper. And if I discover you are involved it won't just be your business you need to worry about.'

'Good luck with that.' Was Teds' parting shot as he left.

'What do you think then Tim?' asked Ray after Ted left.

'I think he was lying about when he last saw Joe, and I would like to wipe that smirk off his face as well.'

'I know what you mean, but we can only do that by wrapping up the case.'

Ray and Tim spent the rest of the day going through the information that the team from Tallenbee had gathered in particular anything relating to Ted. As Ray worked he built up a picture of Ted and who he mixed with, he soon felt even more certain that somewhere Ted was tied in with the death of Joe. Later that afternoon Ray had a call from Jenny to tell him that she had spoken to ballistics and they hoped to have the results for him within the next couple of days. Ray looked over the desk at Tim,

'I think we will spend tonight here, tomorrow we will have another chat with Bloom then make our way home. The team here are on top of things and will keep us informed.'

'Okay sir.'

By the following morning they hadn't turned up anything else from the notes the local officers had on Ted, but Rays' instinct was that he was still crucial to the enquiry. Ray and Tim said goodbye to Robert, who promised them he would keep a couple of officers on the task of checking Ted Bloom. If there was anything else they needed to just get in touch. Ray thanked him and told him they were going to visit Bloom at work on their way out of town. As they entered the bookies Ray saw Ted behind the counter talking to some punters he was laughing and joking with them, when he saw them he moved towards them,

'Have you come to say goodbye then?'

Ray could feel his dislike for the man rise to the surface,

'We have, but I have a feeling we will be talking to you again. You could do better than to think about some of the people you mix with.'

'I'm sure I don't know what you mean.' Ted was smirking even as he spoke.

Ray and Tim left and once they were in the car on the way out of Tallenbee, Tim looked over at Ray.

'He is in on this isn't he sir?'

'Definitely, we just have to prove it, he may not have pulled the trigger but someone is pulling his strings. We just need to find out who.'

Chapter Eight

On the journey back to Lynn Ray found it hard to concentrate, he had a niggling feeling there was something in the background of the case that would open it all up. It was just a case of finding out what, Tim had been fairly quiet on the journey he had been reading through the notes he had made at Tallenbee. His shout of glee shook Ray as he said,

'There is a possibility here sir, which has to be worth looking at.'

'Now you are finished giving me heart failure, tell me what you have found and you're thinking of.'

'I am just wondering reading through the things Ted is supposed to have been involved in and with Joes' liking of gambling, could there be a possibility of a betting scam being behind this. Because as we have said it just seems unlikely that Bloom would write off that amount of money.'

'That sounds a bit farfetched when we are only talking about non-league football isn't it.'

'Maybe that is how they get away with it, being not so high profile it isn't likely to attract too much attention. Also I have come across people in the past who would bet on anything. In actual fact in the pub one night I was amazed to hear two guys bet on which raindrop would reach the bottom of the window first. Anyone listening would have thought the guy that won had got all his numbers up on the lottery. These are the sort of people that the Blooms' of the world just love.'

'Ok Tim it sounds plausible even if a bit farfetched, first thing tomorrow you can spend some time looking in to it, but we will also need some evidence if we are to carry on with that line of enquiry.'

It made Ray feel better that they at least had something to look into, his first job when they returned to the station was to report to Adam Church and bring him up to speed with what they had found out in Tallenbee. The superintendent was unsure as to whether the journey had been worth it, once Ray finished telling him about the interview with Ted Bloom. Then he was really dumbfounded by the suggestion from Tim Jarvis.

'I really cannot see that being likely in such a low profile part of the sport.'

'I understand that sir, but at this moment in time it is at least giving us something to go on. Also having met Ted Bloom I can see the possibilities of him being involved.'

'Okay then but he has only got 48 hours to find something, I need to be convinced we can carry on with this angle to the investigation. You know the next thing I'm going to mention Ray, the finance people have already been on to me so we need to see some progress.'

'Come on sir, it is less than a week we need some time.'

'Yes and I need to see some evidence and progress no

matter how insignificant it may seem. This sounds like clutching at straws.'

Ray knew it was just as well to bite his tongue and count to ten rather than try to answer. Especially when Adam was already mentioning finance, he knew all he could do was his best along with everyone else to get a result.

Ray left the office and headed towards the incident room, to see if Jenny had any good news. On his way he saw that Tim was already at an computer to see what he could find out about a possible betting scam, as he passed by Ray put his head in the door and called out,

'You have got 48 hours to find us something Tim.'

Ray had already moved on before Tim could reply, the news from Jenny was no more encouraging but she did agree that Tim could be on to something.

'It might seem farfetched, but it has happened before at the top level and further down the league there has been suspicion of this sort of thing. The thinking behind it could be if it is lower league, it would be easier to get away with.'

Ray decided the next morning he would visit the local betting shops to see if they had received any unusual betting on recent Lynn Rovers games. He told Jenny that Tim would be tied up on the computer for the next two days at least.

'Tomorrow whilst I am out, I want you to visit Alison again and see if you can find out anymore about Joes' gambling and in particular his past betting. You could also ask how he used to pay off any debts, such as if he had been chased for money in the past. She might feel happier opening up to you and give you some information that I can't get.'

One Good Shot

'You don't mean to tell me your charm is not working do you.' She laughed.

'I just keep my charm for special people. Grieving widows don't come into that category.'

As they were talking some of the collators who were busy working through the mountain of paperwork came in. Ray was quick to react in these situations and just spoke to Jenny as he went out,

'Just let me know if you get anything useful.'

Jenny was used to having to cover things up so took no notice of how brisk Ray spoke. She knew some of the others did wonder about how he addressed her, but she was happy with how things were going between them and wasn't going to do anything to spoil it.

Chapter Nine

On the following morning Ray was astounded by the information given to him by the local bookie. It appeared that bookies were always on the look out for any unusual betting on any sport and despite what the sport authorities would reveal it was a very large problem. The other element involved that made it difficult to get on top of the problem, was that it was worldwide and used the internet as its main source of communication. Over a cup of coffee the bookmaker explained that the big national companies would not get involved with any scam, they were aware of the damage it could do to their business. But that didn't mean it never happened and he couldn't speak for individual operators. The bookmaker also explained that normally any scam would be around sports where individuals took part. This being that it would be easier to arrange the outcome rather than a team sport you would be hoping that the person involved could swing the result as required. It had happened in team sports but not as often. The bookmaker gave Ray an example in that at the moment there was an investigation taking place involving snooker. This showed the bonus of single people, as all it would need was for a player to lose and he would have a certain control over this.

One Good Shot

The bookie felt that the allegations would need some work to prove as most sportsmen got well rewarded but there always was the possibility of someone being greedy. This caught Rays' attention again with the mention of the word greed, which this case seemed to involve quite a lot.

'So how could we go about finding out, if there has been unusual betting on a particular game then?'

'You could start by checking betting shops in a certain area if you had somewhere in mind. Any of the main companies would notify the F.A. if they had taken a lot of different bets or unusual ones. The governing authorities would be the first call they would make. Even if they didn't like admitting the problem, they would very quickly deal with it and if individual athletes were involved they would be dealt by their governing bodies.'

Ray said his thanks and left to return to the station. Thinking how it appeared that things kept coming back with a connection to gambling it seemed to involve Ted Bloom. And from the little he had seen of the man Ray was convinced if there was money on offer Ted would be at the front of the queue. Once he was back in his office he rang the F.A. to see if they had received any reports on betting on Lynn Rovers games recently. He was pleased and surprised to be told that it had been brought to their attention that there had been a lot of money being bet on Lynn the previous weekend, the money had been placed at a couple of independent bookmakers and online there had been generous odds offered for Lynn to lose. This confused Ray at first as Lynn had won the game, it became clearer when it was explained to him that this was how the scam made money. People would be inclined to bet heavily on the good odds then the result would go differently and they would lose their money. The gamblers would not be liable to complain as they would just accept it as the gamble they took, the people behind it all would be careful not to make the outcome seem too suspicious. The man at the F.A told Ray that two major bookmakers in the Tallenbee area had taken large amounts of money on Lynn Rovers to lose the game; they most probably wouldn't have taken any notice except they knew Joe was then playing for them after his injury with Tallenbee. This information made Ray feel he was getting somewhere, so he went to find Jenny in the incident room.

'Hi Jenny any joy with Alison about Joes' past?'

'Not too much sir, but she does seem to think that Ted Bloom has put pressure on Joe in the past. She is still saying that as far as she was concerned it was all cleared up.'

'Right I think I will arrange for Tallenbee police to pick up Bloom, because we really need to speak to him again.'

Ray explained the things he had learned from the bookies and the F.A. then left her to carry on and made his way back to his office to phone Robert, on the way Tim called after him,

'Sir you might want to take a look at this, there is a lot of betting being investigated by the F.A., and looking closer it is not only soccer that has a problem.'

Ray looked at the computer screen that Tim was busy on and said

'Okay Tim spend a bit more time on it to see if our friend Bloom is mentioned at all, but going on what I have been told by the F.A. it seems obvious that some sort of betting scam is behind this.'

While all this was happening in Lynn, Ted Bloom was feeling very uncomfortable with what had been going on in Tallenbee. It started with a phone call he received first thing, in which he was told that he was to be at the Swan Inn in town at lunchtime. Ted was worried immediately because if there was somewhere he felt uncomfortable it was the Swan. The pub was known locally to be where many unsavoury characters met and did business and to show how bad it was, it was the one place that Ted avoided even considering his dodgy dealings. He always felt as though there were several pairs of eyes watching what you were doing. He was told he would be met by someone from the betting syndicate, as they felt he needed reminding about his actions. This made Ted very nervous; he also knew he didn't have an option but to be there.

When he was first approached about getting involved with the syndicate. To offer good odds on several sports, being the sort of person he was, he just saw the money he was offered and didn't see any harm in it. He was more than happy with the money he had made so far, and looked as it being a way to make sure he retired with money behind him. When he heard about Joes' death he realised exactly what was at stake, and straight away he felt he was out of his depth. He felt even more nervous when he saw the mountain of a man who approached him at the table in the pub. Ted just sat open mouthed and listened as the guy explained that his bosses didn't like the fact that Ted had been visited several times by the police. Ted was very flustered as he tried to tell the thug that the police had nothing on him, and as

Ken Ward

far as he was concerned they had left him with no reason to have to return. Ted looked around at the other people in the bar but they all looked away once they saw the size of the person talking to him, it was clearly a case of one wanting to know what was going on but two realising when it was a good idea to not get involved.

'Just make sure it stays that way, or you might just find yourself meeting the same fate Kipper did.'

Ted quickly gulped down the rest of his whiskey as the guy left him at the table. As Ted left the pub he had a feeling that things couldn't get any worse, and he felt that as long as he kept his head down for awhile he would be okay. He walked back to his shop thinking I might even take a holiday. Then as he felt things couldn't get any worse he saw the police car on the side of the street, two officers got out as he approached,

'Mr Bloom would you mind coming with us please?'

'I don't suppose I have much choice do I.'

Ted was taken to Tallenbee police station where Robert Simmons was waiting to question him about betting scams. Teds' first reaction was to brave it out and deny all knowledge of what they were talking about. But when it came down to it, one thing Ted wasn't was brave. So after an attempt at bravado he made up his mind that the only person who could look after him was himself.

'I can most probably help you, but I need some help from you.'

Robert was always loathe to make deals, but he knew that Ray Keane wanted to get this case sewn up so he said,

'Depending on what you can tell us, we will see what we can do for you.'

One Good Shot

This didn't sound brilliant to Ted, but he was slowly realising that he was in deeper than he really wanted to be. He explained that he had been approached by a man in his shop who told Ted, that he knew a way for him to make some money without having to do a lot for it. The idea of making money always appealed to Ted, he went on to explain that all he had to do was arrange for himself, and some other dubious bookies to offer generous odds on certain results of mainly soccer matches, and occasionally other sports. This was sure to attract a lot of bets and the syndicate behind the scam would arrange for the results of the matches to be fixed so that none of the bets would have to be paid out on. Ted then had to go and see Joe about the money he owed him, and tell him that if he followed instructions about some games during the season his debt would be wiped out. It had taken Ted some time but it was no secret as to where Joe had gone once the press release came out about him signing for Lynn. Then it was just a job of getting someone to find out his routine.

'It came as no surprise to me when Joe turned down the offer, but even I didn't expect anyone to get killed over it.'

Robert could tell by the look on Teds' face that the death of Joe really did bother him.

'This is all very helpful Ted, but I will need some names of people involved.'

'Even you must realise these sort of people don't introduce themselves formally.'

'Yes I know but you must have some idea who you were dealing with.'

'The only name I overheard mentioned was someone called French.'

Robert decided to finish up for now and told Ted he could leave the station but not the area, he arranged that officers would keep an eye on him but he would be needed again. After Ted had left Robert rang Lynn to speak to Ray and give him the good news on what they had found out from Ted Bloom. The next thing arranged was for it to be notified that the force was looking for someone called French. It wasn't a lot of help only having the one piece of a name to work with but it was a start.

Chapter Ten

Ray Keane really felt they were getting somewhere when he finished on the phone to Robert Simmons. Firstly he went to see Adam to give him the good news and explained how he hoped that they could tie up the case very soon now that they had some idea of what had happened to cause Joe to be shot. After this he went to the incident room to bring everyone up to speed, on the way he called Tim to follow him. He addressed the room about his conversation with D.I.Simmons in Tallenbee, the list of jobs that needed doing didn't really change as things would still need following up, but he told Tim to stop looking into the betting scams as they would pass the information on to the F.A. who would be interested to investigate that side of things. He told him that if necessary later in the investigation he could go back to it if they felt it would help.

'Once you have passed the info onto them you can start checking our records for anything on someone called French, that is all we have at the moment but you might turn something up. You could start by looking out for any records for snipers that could match the MO for our case. We have to believe this guy is good so he doesn't leave many

Ken Ward

clues, but he may just have slipped up in the past and it just wasn't tied in with anything.'

'Okay sir I'll get right on it.'

The next phone call that Ray received would show how you could go from feeling total euphoria to crestfallen all in the space of a few hours. He had just walked back into his office when the phone rang,

'Hello Ray Keane speaking.'

'Hi Ray its Robert; I'm afraid I'm ringing with some bad news. Two of my lads were keeping tabs on Ted Bloom from when he left the station today; they were keeping an eye on his flat above the bookies.'

'I don't like the sound of this conversation Robert.'

'They never saw anyone going in apart from Bloom, then after about 30 minutes they spotted some guy leaving.'

Robert went onto explain that the two officers went up to investigate and discovered the door open, they found Ted Bloom laying on his living room floor having been shot. They called for backup and searched the area but whoever they saw leaving was long gone. The officers couldn't really give any description of the man except that he was nondescript. This showed that you couldn't always use eye witnesses' accounts, about descriptions. The police had it drilled into them at training school that you should always take note of things. But if two officers now had a description of a nondescript person then what could the public be expected to be able to add. Ray thought that tied in with their descriptions of their killer, the police doctor had been called and he confirmed that Ted had died as a result of a bullet to the head.

'Okay Robert, you deal with the case at your end, but I think we have to treat it as being connected with our case.'

One Good Shot

Ray went back to the incident room to tell the team what he had just heard. There was a groan from everyone as they realised that they were now back to square one, but they now had two bodies. As Ray went to leave the room a young officer handed him an envelope saying,

'This just arrived for you Sir.'

'Thanks lad.'

Ray knew it was going to be the ballistics report he had been waiting for with the details of the bullet that had killed Joe. He tore open the envelope and read the information, they could tell Ray that it had been a .50 bullet and that it had been fired from a high powered rifle. The report only confirmed things that Ray already knew and also explained that as no-one had heard a shot it suggested that the rifle had a silencer fitted. This again pointed towards it being a professional as to have fired the distance and with the accuracy was hard enough it would have been made more difficult because a silencer made a gun more awkward to handle. Rays' next job was to contact Tallenbee to find out more details of the death of Ted Bloom, Robert told him that the initial impressions from the men at the scene was that a handgun had been used and that the person who used it knew what they were doing as the was very little mess made. Robert agreed that it most probably tied in with Joes' death as only one bullet had been fired suggesting a professional hit.

'Has the wife been of any help to you at all?'

'Not really.' Replied Ray, "I t does seem to be that she didn't know what was going on, and also she certainly was taken back when I told her how much debt Joe was in for."

'You better keep an eye out for her though, because it is always possible that she could become a target.'

'I know it is a worry but we will keep a close eye on her, I will talk to you again soon.'

Once Ray finished on the phone he slumped back in his chair feeling utterly deflated. He didn't really believe that Alison was a target of these people, but he knew it was his responsibility to keep an open mind. He now sat thinking how from a few hours ago of seeming to have made a breakthrough in the case, it now felt as if they were no further forward than they had been at 3.15 on the previous Saturday. He knew that they could do with a lucky break, as well as a lot of hard work it was amazing how much detection was completed through some good luck.

Chapter Eleven

Whilst Ray was hoping he wouldn't have to wait too long for the lucky break. Alison Kipper was trying to come to terms with the events of the last week. Firstly there was the grief at having heard of the death of Joe, and then she had slowly come to terms with the information from the police into how much debt Joe had been in. The funeral had been arranged for the following Wednesday, and so far no-one from the press had managed to find out where she was staying and for this she had the police to thank. She realised that they would be able to find out when the funeral was but felt she would deal with that on the day. Her parents had been very supportive, and rallied round when they realised the problems that were mounting up. With the help of the police, Alison had started to understand the situation better and the way things were going, the police were also helping explain the possibility of getting things sorted out. In as much as she had loved Joe she had always known what he was like over the gambling. She now felt she had to do her best to try and get things organized so it didn't affect her any more than necessary. Her first thoughts were to get through the funeral, and then she wanted to sort out her own finances. She didn't want the people who were behind the killing finding out too much of what was going on. As far as she was concerned it was Joe who owed the money, and if the police could find out who was behind it all then it shouldn't affect her. Only she knew it would leave emotional scars that were for her to deal with. Alison knew it would be difficult but the first thing was to get herself sorted, since the news of Joe's death Alison had not really taken any time over herself or her appearance. She couldn't remember going so long without doing her hair or make-up and had spent the time slouching around in a tracksuit this just wasn't her.

'Are you alright love?' her mum said as she came into the room.

'Yes mum, I'm going to have a shower and make myself presentable.'

'Okay love, take your time you'll feel better in yourself afterwards.'

Alison left her mum in the room and went upstairs, she knew her parents were only doing their best, but Alison knew she was the only one who could sort herself out and get through the coming days and weeks. Amazingly as soon as she got in the shower and let the hot water flow over her, she started to feel better, even though she knew it would be difficult deep down she knew she could get through this and get her life back afterwards. Even though Joe had been an idiot over the gambling he would never have done anything to harm her. She now realised that an agreement they had made when they sold the house was now going to be very helpful. That was that they decided the proceeds from the sale and consequently the new house had all been put in Alison's' name so at least she felt this would be of help. After her shower Alison rang to speak to Ray Keane, he wasn't available but the officer told her he would be given a message to ring her as soon as possible. While she waited for him to return her call Alison got herself dressed and did her hair and make-up, when she looked in the mirror she was surprised by how much better she looked. Alison was determined that she would look her best for the funeral as she felt this would be what Joe would have wanted. She was getting ready to go into the town with her mum to sort out last minute funeral arrangements when Ray phoned from the police station.

'Hello Alison I understand you want to talk to me.'

'Yes mainly to ask about any arrangements you had in mind for Wednesday.'

'We will be at the funeral one out of respect. But we will also be keeping a close eye on any unexpected or unexplained guests, I realise this will not be easy because there will be a lot of people there to pay their respects. It is just possible that someone from Joes' past might be there who could help us out.'

'I'm sure I can leave things in your capable hands, so I will see you on Wednesday.'

Ray already had plans in place to police the funeral, he knew it would be busy with all friends and fans from Tallenbee and in the short time he had lived in Lynn he had become popular. Ray was also hoping to spot some unsavoury characters from his past as he was sure that Joe had come across several people like this in the casinos. Even though Ray had attended a lot of funerals because of his job, he didn't like going to them. This was really a personal thing; his dads' funeral had been a big affair because of the fact that he had been killed during a raid on a drug dealer's house. It had been splashed across the papers at the time that Neil Keane had been an innocent bystander who had been gunned down by one of the drug dealers as he tried to escape from the police, the press had reported that Neil had been a have go hero as he had tried to stop one of the crooks from leaving the scene. Ray knew from talking to the officers who attended the scene it was more likely that he had just been in the wrong place at the wrong time. All Ray knew was that his fathers' death was not totally in vain as all the gang of dealers had been caught and were now serving long prison sentences. This encouraged Ray in his career in the knowledge that with hard work some crooks did get what they deserved. When Ray had attended the funeral he was overwhelmed by the crowds. What he found difficult to accept was the fact he knew very few of them. All he could do was support his mother through the day and he knew she was proud of her husband this was important to him. Now his mother was in a home suffering from alzehiemers and going on the lack of visitors, he thought when her time came the only mourners were likely to be the staff from the home and him.

Ray had arranged for Jenny to accompany him to the funeral and other officers would be assigned to attend outside to see if they could spot anyone unusual. Wednesday arrived and to Ray it was a typical funeral day cloudy with a threat of rain. Ray and Jenny got to the church in good time and even he was taken aback by the crowds that were there. He had realised that is was going to be one of the most high profile funerals there had been in the area for a while. Even though Joe was young he had an enormous following of fans due to his achievements in the game, also the fact that he had played for a successful team not far from Lynn meant more fans than expected had

One Good Shot

travelled to pay their respects. The local press seemed to be in competition with the nationals to get the most photos, on the way into the church Ray stopped and spoke to Tim,

'Get it sorted with one of the local boys can you, that we get copies of all photos they take.'

'Okay sir I'll talk to one of them that I know.'

'That will be handy see you back at the station later.'

The church was packed and the funeral passed off as well as could be expected, Ray always felt there was an extra sadness to a funeral when it was a young person and from his point of view he felt it was harsh that there appeared to still be no sensible reason for Joe's death. When he spotted Alison at the front of the church it made him feel even more determined to find out why and who had killed Joe. The funeral passed in a blur and as the coffin was removed from the church there was light everywhere as flashbulbs of all the press appeared to go off simultaneously. Then when the family left to make their way to the crematorium for a private ceremony as if on cue the clouds deposited an enormous amount of rainfall. Ray thought this summed up how people were feeling as they left.

After the funeral Ray and Jenny went back to the station and Ray organized a meeting of the team in the incident room, it took about 30 minutes for everyone to get together and Adam also appeared.

'Right everyone I want an extra 10% of effort on this because I want to be able to tell Alison Kipper who killed her husband and that we have arrested them.'

Adam took to the front of the room and addressed the team,

'Firstly thank you for the effort that you have all put in so far, but we do need to start getting information that I can show the budgeting people because they are already on to me about the cost.'

This brought an audible groan from the room, Adam put up his hand,

'I know but we all know we are being watched constantly, so keep up the good work and get me the information I need so this case can be wrapped up satisfactorily.'

Adam looked at Ray and nodded as he left the room. Ray turned to his team and said,

'Right you all know what you need to do so off you go and let's get this wrapped up.'

Though there had been a large number of people from outside of Lynn at the funeral no-one had stood out to any of the officers observing proceedings. Ray hoped that when they got some of the pictures back he could send them to Robert, and hope that some of his officers might recognise someone. He was passed a message as he left to go to his office. It was phoned through from Alison to say thank you for the help with the funeral, and to let him know that her and her parents were going to spend some time at a holiday flat her dad owned. It was along the coast at Blakeney and would be quiet at this time of year. She had added that she felt this would be good for her and Ray had her mobile number if he needed to contact her. Ray was hopeful that the next time he would need to speak to Alison would be with good news that they had got a result. He could fully understand her need for peace and quiet and knew that initially it had been the one thing that helped him cope with the death of his wife.

Chapter Twelve

The lucky break that Ray had been wishing for came in the early hours of the next morning. And as could be usual in police work it was something that appeared to be totally unconnected with the case that was to prove a real help.

Two things happened and due to good work by the officers involved the link was made to help Ray and his team.

The first incident was when two officers stopped a car on a motorway that bypassed Tallenbee in the early hours of the morning. Initially they stopped the car they were following because he had no rear lights, this could have happened to anyone. The officers approached the car to speak to the driver, the first thing they noticed was that guy seemed at ease talking to them most people would automatically get nervous when stopped by the police. After informing him about his faulty lights they took his details as a matter of course, as they still had some of their shift left they told the driver they would follow him home. He had told them this was where he was headed, once back in the car one of the officers said,

'That guy's name is familiar does it ring any bells with you?'

'Yes now you mention it, it was on a memo that some officers from Norfolk wanted to speak to someone called French. Radio it in and we will pick him up from his home.'

'What if he makes a run for it?'

'It's unlikely he seemed calm enough when we spoke to him, so I don't think he was suspicious at all.'

As it happened Jack never gave it a thought to make a run for it, he didn't think he had anything to worry about. It was surely bad luck that his rear lights had been out, but the officers didn't seem unduly concerned by it so he felt confident he would be okay. At the same time that this was happening and the two officers were advised to bring Jack French in for questioning, Terry Jennings was remembering something from the Saturday afternoon which was going to lead to another slice of luck for Ray. It was to do with a hat that he remembered the person in the trees had been wearing, he realised just what he had seen when he saw someone on telly wearing a similar hat, and even though it had been warm he thought it was strange that they had been wearing an Aussie style hat without the corks. Obviously what Terry didn't know was that Jack always wore this type of hat. Terry phoned the police station and was told that they would pass the message on to Inspector Keane, and he would contact him.

When Ray got into his office the next morning he couldn't believe his messages and what they were telling him. His first phone call was to Robert in Tallenbee who confirmed that two of his guys had picked up someone called Jack French. Even though he was refusing to answer any questions Robert told Ray he felt they had enough to

One Good Shot

go and get a search warrant for his house. Robert had been suspicious of Jack in that he immediately gave them the name of a solicitor. He was extremely calm which Robert had learnt over the years could be a sign of someone hiding something. Ray was happy for the search to be done as long as Robert thought he could get the warrant organized.

'Tell them to look out for an Aussie style hat during the search please Robert.'

'That's a bit weird isn't, I would have told the team to be looking for a rifle and a handgun, and now you want them to look for a hat?'

Ray explained about the phone call from Terry and he added that at first he hadn't totally trusted his judgement as a witness but it was at least a starting point. Also it possibly could be used as a start to tie French in with being above the soccer ground at the right time. Ray felt that even though it seemed they were getting somewhere, he just needed time to think things over without any distractions. He went to the incident room and saw Jenny at her desk,

'I'm going out for a while, ring me if you must.'

'Okay Sir.'

It was taken as a matter of course that Ray would go out and have time alone while working a case; it was accepted by his team. To Ray it was one of the local pleasures to be able to leave the hustle and bustle of the station behind and within ten minutes be beside the river Ouse, and enjoy some peace and quiet. He walked along the quayside knowing exactly where he was heading, he would go into the cafe and get a coffee to take out and then go and sit by the river. As Ray sat drinking his coffee he was just like many of the other locals who sat by the river in good weather. Most of the tourists had finished their stays for the year so it was quite peaceful. Ray looked around him at the area, for many years now there had been ambitious plans by several companies to renovate the quayside. These plans always revolved around the main idea to build a marina and attract more people; there was always a reason why it never happened. The latest idea was to demolish the massive grain silos' and then for a hotel chain to build. For once Ray thought this was one venture that could actually bear fruit and become reality.

Ray sat and let his mind wander back over the previous week's business. He started to try and think logically forward over everything they had learnt so far and how it was possibly inter linked. As he placed his thoughts in order it just seemed more and more too difficult to comprehend that Joe Kipper had been killed just because he had refused to fix the score of a soccer match. Though understanding the minds of a criminal he knew anything was possible. Ray was just finishing his coffee when his mobile rang; when he saw it was Jenny calling he knew she must have thought it was important to disturb his peace and quiet,

'Hi Jenny what have you got for me?'

'The D.I. from Tallenbee just rang to say that they finished the initial search of Jack Frenchs' house and there is no sign of any weapons or a hat. The message said that they were about to start a more thorough search and would let us know what it turns up.'

'Okay I'm on my way back and I'll ring Robert to arrange another visit.'

On his way back he decided that he would go and see this French character for himself and he would take Lisa with him and she could go and look round both Jacks' house and Ted Blooms' flat to see if she could find anything to tie them in with the shooting. He felt that her view on things might be different as she had been involved with the searches that had been made in the area at the beginning. He also realised that he could well be clutching at straws, but you just never knew.

Chapter Thirteen

It was agreed that Ray and Lisa would go to Tallenbee, Ray would sit in on the interview with Jack French and Lisa would do her stuff, first she would go to Jacks' house. Then she was going to take a look at the crime scene at Ted Blooms' flat. They left immediately and made the journey in good time, once in Tallenbee, Ray and Lisa went to the police station and it was arranged for a local P.C.to go with her and show her the way to both places she wanted to visit. Ray made his way to the office to meet Robert,

'Afternoon Robert, how you doing?'

'Not too bad thanks'

'Has he given you anything to go on?'

'Not yet, but listening to him I'm not surprised. This guy is certainly a professional. He is a very cool customer.'

'Oh well, we will just have to talk to him more then. He can't be a lot different to all the others we have dealt with in our time.'

'Yes I agree but all that does is make me feel old. If you want to come with me, you can have a look at him before we go in and talk to him.'

Ray followed Robert out and into the interview areas of the station; they walked into a room with a long mirrored wall. Ray looked through and thought how calm the guy looked considering the fact that they thought he had killed two people, and who knew possibly many more.

While Ray was getting his first look at Jack French and preparing to interview him, Lisa was arriving at his house. She got herself suited up and made her way indoors, the house was a hive of activity and the police were being thorough, carpets and floorboards were pulled up, and cupboards and wardrobes were being searched. The P.C. who had brought Lisa over introduced her to the D.S. in charge of the search.

'Hello I'm Lisa, forensics from Lynn.'

'Hi I'm Jim, my job is to oversee this lot.' He replied as he swept his arm around the front room. "Anywhere you particularly want to look at?"

'No just a general look here, I would think if I'm going to find any major clues it will be at the bookies if this guy killed him. I would think here it is more likely for you to find evidence to tie him in with everything. Paperwork is liable to be your biggest help. Lisa made her way cautiously around the house; it could have been anyone's house, there was nothing to suggest otherwise. In the corner of the living room was a large screen television and stereo system, the collection of D.V.D's on the shelves gave very little away about a person nor did the books. She felt a bit more hopeful in the bedroom where in a wardrobe they had found two pairs of trainers with plain soles. This tied in with there being no real prints at the crime scene in Lynn, Lisa bagged both pairs up and let Jim know she was taking them.

From Jack Frenchs' house Lisa was taken across the town to the bookies, this flat was the total opposite of the house, it was messy and untidy. Takeaway pots were all lying on the coffee table in the middle of the room. Lisa stood and looked around before speaking,

'Was this mess made during the killing?'

'No I have visited here several times and it always looks like this, in fact this is reasonably tidy compared to how I have seen it.' replied a young officer.

'Right I better have a look round and see if I can find anything to help us out.'

Ray was now getting ready to interview Jack, without knowing that Lisa was on the other side of town about to find something that would give Ray his second lucky break in the case. Ray entered the interview room and straight away took a dislike to Jack French and the smarmy guy sitting beside him. Robert started the tape machine going and both of them sat down. After the formalities of introduction of those present for the tape. The solicitor spoke immediately.

'I am Rick Kirby and am representing Mr French; I would like to say that my client doesn't understand why he is here. Your officers stopped him for a defective rear light on his car and now you want to question him about two murders.'

Ray looked across at the solicitor then said,

'We would like to ask Mr French some questions after his name was mentioned to us in an investigation.'

'So you are basing your allegations on a name being mentioned, I don't think there is a lot more to be said do you?'

Ray was about to respond when there was a knock at the door,

'Come in,' called Robert.

A young P.C. put his head round the door,

'Can I have a word Sir?'

Robert left the room,

'Lisa Hall from forensics has just phoned Sir, she has found something interesting at Ted Blooms' and has asked can you arrange to get a hair sample from French for her to compare she is on her way back now.'

Robert re-entered the room and informed Mr Kirby and Jack French that they would be keeping him in custody and would like a hair sample. Ray noticed a flicker of emotion pass across Jacks' face at this statement, and then he appeared to gather himself and very smugly said,

'Ok then let's get this over with then and afterwards you can apologize.'

After they had taken the hair sample and French was back in the cell, Ray had an anxious wait for Lisa to return and explain what she had found.

Lisa had been unsure that she was going to find anything in the mess that was Ted Blooms' flat, it was a mess throughout. She looked in the kitchen but there wasn't a clear surface anywhere, the bedroom wasn't much better but she decided that she might be able to glean some forensics such as hair samples from in there. The lucky break that everyone had been hoping for came in the living room, as with all the other rooms it was a tip but on the back of the sofa Lisa found two or three blonde hairs, Ted Bloom was known to have had very short grey hair. Lisa put the hair in a bag then phoned the station as she made her way out of the mess and got back in the car asking the P.C. to take her back.

Chapter Fourteen

Lisa made the journey back to the police station doing her best to contain her excitement, she had learnt over the years to not believe things until she was proved correct. But she also realised how important this case was for Ray and was keen to help in any way she could. As Lisa entered the police station Ray and Robert were waiting to hear what she had found out, trying her best to be casual she held up the bag with the hair in it.

'I need to get back to the lab so I can check these for a match with the samples you took from his head.'

Ray saw the look in her eyes that showed she felt they had something to work on.

'Okay Lisa we will make our way back to Lynn for you to do your stuff. Robert can you arrange to give our friend in there the use of the facilities here and hold him for as long as possible, also step up the search at his house to see if they can find anything else.'

'No problem the pleasure will be all mine, let me know if you get a match on the hair.'

As Lisa and Ray were saying goodbye and getting ready to leave the police station a P.C. came rushing in holding a large evidence bag in his hand.

One Good Shot

'What have you found then?' asked Robert

'It is a hat sir.'

He held the bag up for them to see it properly and apart from the fact that it didn't have any corks hanging from it, it looked just like an Aussie hat as had been described by Terry Jennings, Ray just looked at the others and smiled.

'Well it looks as though things are falling into place doesn't it.'

'Certainly does.' Replied Robert.

'Right Lisa if you take the hair samples and a swab from inside the hat, then go back to Lynn to do your stuff. I will stay here and see what else we can dig up.'

Lisa did what she needed to do, then it was arranged for her to be taken back to Lynn and Ray was going to ring and speak to Jenny to let her know what was happening. This would also give him the brief chance to speak to Jenny and make sure she was okay. Even though she always told him that she was happy with their relationship he would get times when he was insecure and worry that she would want more and he would not be able to give her this. The time with Jenny since the death of his wife had been very good and in particular the last three years where they had been seeing more of each other, had lifted him and he didn't want to lose that feeling. He told Lisa he was also going to organize it for Tim to travel back to Tallenbee with the officer as Ray felt that if they were both here it would help them in tying up the case, Ray was happy that the team in Lynn could handle things that end. Ray followed Robert into his office and sat down,

'We need to look into his bank details and see if there is anything on his computer.'

Ken Ward

'I'll get some lads onto it straight away, but it would not surprise not to find a lot because this guy is certainly careful.'

'Yes I know, but there is normally a trail somewhere. Someone pays for his services and also someone must get in touch to let him know what they want doing.'

Ray leant back in the chair and sighed,

'I think I would like to have a look at house, just to get a feel of the place.'

'Okay Ray I'll get someone to take you over there, the guys are still searching, maybe you could give them a hand.' Laughed Robert.

Ray smiled and left the office saying,

'I'll go and get a coffee until you can arrange for someone to take me over there.'

'Okay Ray, I'll speak to you later.'

Ray was just finishing his coffee and comparing the view from the window to his office in Lynn. Again he just felt that he could be in any office anywhere, whereas in Lynn the view was unique as far as Ray thought. His office overlooked the park and war memorial which always seemed to have a sense of peace to Ray. He looked up as a W.P.C approached the table,

'Hello Sir I'm Sue Hawkins I'm told you need taking to Jack Frenchs' house.'

'That's right but let's drop the Sir bit, it is Inspector Keane, so come on Sue lets go and see what we can find.'

When they arrived at the house it was starting to resemble an empty shell, all the carpets had been pulled up and cupboards emptied. Ray went in and initially went from room to room just looking at the thorough job that

One Good Shot

was being undertaken. He stopped when he entered the living room,

'Have you found a computer at all?' He asked no one in particular.

'Not yet, we haven't but there are a lot of small cupboards where you would be able to hide things.'

'Okay you keep going through things down here, I'm going to look in the bedroom.'

In the bedroom was a small desk in one corner with very little on it, and a few books stacked in a pile on the floor beside the bed. Ray started by looking through the draws in the desk they were all empty, the one thing that struck Ray was that French must have been a loner there were no photos anywhere that he could see. Ray realised that this would fit in with a profile off a professional killer as it would be unusual for such a person to have family or close friends as what would you tell them about your life. Ray picked up the books and scanned the spines there was nothing special just run of the mill thrillers, he shook the books to see if anything fell out but again no luck. He moved over to the wardrobe and was surprised by the lack of clothes it really looked as though someone did not live here all the time; this convinced him that Jack had somewhere else he lived and maybe worked from. He poked around the wardrobe and was rewarded by the sound of a loose panel at the back.

'Someone bring me a crowbar up here.' He shouted down the stairs,

Sue ran up the stairs with a crowbar and a hammer in her hands, Ray pried the panel away and smiled then inwardly cheered as he saw a laptop.

'Sue can you bring me an evidence bag please.' Ray

asked as he held the laptop carefully. He placed the laptop in the bag and said,

'I'm going to stay here and see if there is anything else, can you get that back to the station and get someone to start looking through the files to see if there is anything of use on them.'

'Right away do you want me to come back for you?'

'Yes you can do, I think these guys will be here for a while because there does seem to be plenty of places to hide things.'

Ray spent the next hour basically taking the bedroom to pieces hoping to find some sort of paper trail, after going through all the cupboards and taking them to pieces he decided that anything else was not hidden here, he made his way downstairs just as Sue got back from the station.

'Right lads keep pulling this place apart if needed brick by brick, I'm going back to the station to see what French has to say about the hidden computer. Remember we are looking for any bank statements and we are still looking for a weapon we think he used.'

As Ray was going out of the door he turned back,

'Just a thought, keep an eye open for any keys that don't fit locks here, it is looking to me more like that he had somewhere else to keep things because this doesn't look to me like a house that is lived in all the time.'

Chapter Fifteen

While the team had been busy at Jack Frenchs', another team of officers were at the bookies. There was also a team searching the flat upstairs. Because in as much as Ted had given the police some information, he had still been involved in the betting scam. This meant he would have also been paid for his part in the matter. The computers in the shop didn't yield any information, except that business had been reasonably good and Ted was making a comfortable living. It was always a mystery to the police that someone who was making a reasonable living could still be swayed by the idea of making some easy money. True once they had met Ted you could sense that greed was obviously a big motivator in his life. The officers who had interviewed him initially felt the betting scam and his connection to it had to have been down to greed. The laptop that they discovered in his flat would hopefully lead them to something more interesting. The laptop had been hidden but not very successfully it was just pushed underneath the sofa. Because Ted was not as tidy or professional as Jack obviously was, they found several bank statements lying around which were showing very healthy figures. A quick glance showed regular payments of £10, 000 being deposited every couple of months. And looking back quickly it had been going on for about a year. The officer conducting the search radioed through to the station and it was organized for the laptop to be brought back to the station. They were told to send back the statements they had found as well, then to keep on searching. The laptop would be examined at the station along with the computer from Jacks'; it was always possible there would be some information that would cross between both computers to tie Ted in with Jack.

The specialist team of officers had already started work on the computer which Ray had found at Jacks'; but so far they had drawn a blank. This just proved how careful Jack was. Ray just knew from experience that everyone slipped up somewhere, it was just a case of finding something. Ray was pacing up and down the corridor while the tech guys were doing their stuff. After an hour of waiting while they worked through the files Ray went to see Robert,

'This is doing me no good at all. I'm going to go back to Frenchs' house and help the search team there.'

'Okay Ray I'll let you know if we find anything. But you don't need to tell me about the frustration, it is just a case of patience till we find the clue we need, it will be there somewhere.'

Ray knew this but at least at the house he would feel he was doing something constructive. Once he arranged transport to the house he was not surprised to see that the floorboards were now being lifted up. There was also a ladder up to the loft and lights had been rigged up, there were two officers working their way through boxes that were up there.

'Any luck with finding any different keys yet?'

One Good Shot

'No not yet, but there are still places we are finding to search. There appears to be just as many hiding places as rooms here.'

Ray made his way upstairs and into what was obviously meant as a spare room. The room had been given a quick search but the more detailed work had not reached here yet. He made a start on a chest of drawers in the corner. As he moved to reach something on the back of the chest, Ray got another lucky break; he felt the floorboards give slightly underfoot. He called down the stairs,

'Someone bring me a crowbar up here please.'

The officer who came up helped Ray move the chest to one side and they worked the floorboards loose. Underneath was a pleasant surprise for Ray, hidden was another laptop and an envelope with some money and keys in. Ray didn't want to waste time going back to the station, so he rang Robert and asked him to speak to French and see what he had to say about the other keys. He also told Robert he would send the laptop back. As he finished on the phone there was a sudden shout from the loft, one of the lads came down with a handgun and some bullets that had been taped to the side of the water tank. Ray was starting to feel good about things and that they were making progress. Ray bagged the gun and ammo and decided that he now had enough evidence here that his next move had to be to speak to Jack French himself. It seemed that suddenly things were moving at a faster pace. Ray stopped himself and took a deep breath he needed to keep his emotions in check he knew when he was face to face with French he needed to keep calm. Ray was hoping to use any momentum he could to rattle French, and get to the bottom of the case as soon

Ken Ward

as possible. When Ray got back French was in an interview room with his solicitor, Robert met him as he came in,

'He is certainly rattled by you finding that laptop and those keys.'

'He is going to be shaken to the core now then.'

Ray showed Robert the gun and ammo. Robert smiled,

'This will make the next few minutes interesting then Ray.'

Ray walked into the room and Jack looked up with a smug grin on his face and said,

'I hope you lot haven't made too much mess at my home, I do like it to be tidy.'

Ray sat down then spoke,

'I don't think we will have to make much more mess. Not now we have found this.'

He slid the evidence bag with the gun in along the table. Throughout his career Ray had seen it happen many times when someone who was very smug sat while the colour drained out of their face. Jacks' shoulders slumped and all of a sudden he didn't look so self assured, it appeared as though all the life had been sucked out of him.

'So can you explain why there was a handgun in your house? And why it was hidden in your loft?'

Before Jack even had time to think of an answer, Ray continued.

'I'm sure that when we pass these bullets to forensic, they are going to tell us they match the bullet found in Ted Blooms' body. And before you get any idea that I am feeling sorry for him, I just want you to know the only people I feel sorry for are Joe Kipper and in particular his wife Alison.'

One Good Shot

Ray watched as Jack did his best to gather his composure. After a brief moment he appeared to be ready to carry on talking. Ray just knew he had got him rattled and knew this was his chance to get the information he needed.

Chapter Sixteen

Jack was a professional, but he also knew when the odds were stacked against him. He had sat quietly for a few minutes, after Ray had put the gun on the table. He was impassive while Ray had finished his speech, which left Jack with very little to say in his defence. Like most career criminals his first thought was too look for someone else to blame, and look after himself as much as possible.

'You have to realise I was only doing a job. I got told what to do and then got paid for it.'

'Paid very well from the look of your house. And I take it I would be right in thinking that you got paid more than Ted Bloom?'

'I wouldn't know what anyone else got paid, that isn't how these things work.'

Before anyone could speak again Rick Kirby spoke up.

'I think I should have a word with my client before we carry on.'

Jack looked at the solicitor and Ray thought he saw a look of distaste in his eyes. He then said,

'I know I am going to need legal representation, but if you would like to just sit and listen. I'll say what I want to.'

One Good Shot

It was then Robert who spoke and if the solicitor was shocked by Jacks' comments, he was even more taken aback by what he next heard.

'I think Mr. Kirby that your client has a point. And when we get the time I will also like to ask you some questions about who hired you, as I have a feeling that it may tie you into the case as well.'

There were now two people in the room who were feeling distinctly more uncomfortable than they had been thirty minutes earlier. Ray was in no mood to let this opportunity to get the confession he needed pass by. Ray had always been the sort of officer who knew and accepted that you had to move with the times so he had learnt from others over the years about such things as profilers being used, and also he had studied body language with specialists and he could tell from the exchanges that had just taken place, that Jack knew he needed the solicitor but that he also realised that Mr. Kirby was there to not only protect his rights but someone else who was obviously in the background.

'Right Jack we will talk about Ted Bloom in a moment but before we go any further I must inform you. I am arresting you for the murders of Joe Kipper and Ted Bloom, you do not have to say anything but it may harm your defence if you don't mention when questioned, something which you later rely on in court. Anything you do say may be given in evidence. Do you understand this?'

'Yes I know.'

'So let us get on then shall we, can you explain how you killed Joe Kipper and why?'

'Why is the easy part I was told to. That is what I do,

Ken Ward

I went to the hill above the soccer ground and it was just a case of waiting for my chance.'

'Did you not think of the possibility that you might have hurt someone else?'

Just briefly the smug grin reappeared on Jacks' face.

'That would never have happened; I'm too good for that. That is why I get paid the amount I do.'

'We will come back to what you get paid soon. First where is the gun you used for the hit? And just so you are aware we have found some unidentified keys at your house. So I take it they have something to do with it?'

Jack took a deep breath then continued.

'They are for a flat on the other side of town. You will find the rifle there and all my payment details.'

This brought an exhale of breath from Rick.

'Do you have something to say Mr. Kirby?' Asked Robert.

Rick just shook his head and Ray continued.

'Right let us have the address, and we will get some officers over there. Because in as much as you know what trouble in, we might as well get things cleared up as soon as possible.'

Once Jack gave them the details, Ray suspended the interview and followed Robert out of the room.

'How did you know that Kirby was tied up in all this, Robert?'

'Experience I suppose, French gave us his name as soon as he was brought in. But Mr. Kirby turned up while we were still getting French through the custody suite, which suggests to me that someone was keeping an eye on the situation.'

One Good Shot

'So shouldn't we get a different solicitor then?'

'Yes we will but as Mr. French is willing to talk to us, without using his solicitor, we will carry on and let Mr. Kirby sweat then we will talk to him as well.'

'I can only go along with your experience and agree to carry on as it feels we could have the breakthrough we need.'

Robert left Ray in the corridor to pass the address details on to the desk sergeant. He would send some of the officers from Jacks' house to the flat. They would continue to search both properties to ensure nothing was missed. It was now a case of making sure that the case against Jack was watertight. It was going to be a help that Jack appeared to be willing to tell them everything but they needed to make sure nothing went wrong when the case went to court.

They re-entered the room and continued the interview.

'So who actually pays you then Jack?'

'That is something I never know. I work by reputation, if someone wants to hire me they find me and all contact is carried out by phone.'

'You are telling us that you never know who you are working for?'

'There is no need, as long as I get paid. That is all that I am interested in.'

'So what would you do if you didn't get paid?'

'I never thought about it. It has never happened; I know I am taking the chances. As is occurring now I face the consequences if something goes wrong. Also I think it highly unlikely that someone would go to the trouble of hiring me, and then try to get away without paying me. They must realise if they found me I could find them.'

Ken Ward

'That sounds plausible, but surely you realise that in as much as we have you. I would really like to get the people involved at the top of the organization.'

'All I can say to you then is good luck, because I don't see that I can help you with that.'

Ray looked over at Robert and shrugged.

'I think for now we should extend our hospitality to Mr. French and Mr. Kirby. While we see what else we can find out.'

'Good idea it might help Mr. French remember something that might help us.'

Jack simply shrugged and stood up to be taken back to the cells. Whereas Rick Kirby was sitting open mouthed just looking at both detectives.

'Why would you want to lock me up?'

Robert replied,

'Well I find it hard to trust solicitors who I have never met before. And also I think it is quite likely you can throw some light on the matter in hand, to help us clear things up.'

Rick sank back down in his chair and seemed resolved to accepting his fate. As both men were led away, Robert turned to Ray.

'Now the work really starts to make sure we can keep the two of them here and find out who is behind this.'

'Do you think Kirby is involved then?'

'If not directly, there has to be a good chance he knows something that could help us. What next for you then Ray?'

'I will go and meet the team at this flat that French has and see what we can find.'

One Good Shot

'Okay, let me know if you need anything else. Then we will see about getting this case wrapped up ready for the prosecution people to get their teeth into.'

While Ray had been busy with the interviews. Tim had been working hard finding out what background information he could on Jack French. Once Ray had passed the name onto him he had been trawling through the police records to see if there was any sign of him. This had drawn a blank, which only proved that he had been careful and there had been no reason for the police to talk to him. Next he started research into his background this was where it became interesting. Jack had joined the army straight from school, and his army record was impressive. He had won many shooting awards while going through training and he had done two tours of duty in Northern Ireland. His skill as a marksman had not gone unnoticed. Then there had been problems when he returned from his second tour, he had got involved in an argument with a senior officer and had lashed out breaking the man's' jaw this was not something that the services were happy with so Jack was discharged. It appeared that after this he went abroad and worked as a hired gun for anyone who would pay, this seemed to be what his life was now about and Tim wondered if they would ever know how many people he had killed. He passed this all on to Ray as he knew that it always helped in a case to know as much as possible about everyone involved. As extra information always helped, Tim had looked into what if anything was known about Ted Bloom. Again there was no police record but he had been spoken to several times by officers investigating dealings of crooked bookmakers. His history was that he had helped his dad run an on course betting company and then had put his own money in to open his shop. The only thing noticeable in the records was that all officers who had had dealings with him had recorded comments that they didn't feel he was the sort of person to be trusted.

Chapter Seventeen

Ray was convinced after speaking with Robert that Rick Kirby was involved somehow. He agreed with Robert that it was weird how he had turned up at the police station, within moments of the arresting officers bringing in Jack French. This pointed towards someone who was tracking Jacks' movements must have contacted Mr. Kirby. As he was about to leave the station he stopped and spoke to the desk sergeant,

'Could you please find out for me who hired Mr. Kirby as solicitor for Jack French?'

The sergeant looked up with a grin which suggested he knew something.

'Mr. Kirby's' client list is fairly full of most of our neighbourhoods unsavoury characters Sir. Also he works for himself so I don't know how much we could find out, leave it with me and I'll try some contacts and see what appears.'

Ray spoke back over his shoulder as he went out the door,

'Thanks for that.'

When Ray got to the flat it looked as though an organized demolition was taking place. Floorboards were being lifted and partition walls were being taken apart. Ray found the officer in charge and asked if they had found anything.

'So far Sir, we have a pile of bank statements also a rifle and ammunition.'

'Good that was the main things I was hoping you would unearth. Keep looking you never know what other surprises you might come across.'

Ray went and sat in the lounge and started reading through the bank statements. It was obvious that Jack must have been good, which Ray found galling to have to admit that a killer was good at his profession. As he currently had £750,000 in his bank. The last two credits were for £200,000 and £50,000. Ray was guessing that one was for the killing of Joe and that the lesser amount was for removing Ted Bloom from the equation. The payments previous to this went back over a period of two years; this led Ray to thinking about who else Jack had killed. He made a mental note to ask this very question when he got back. As he made his way through the mountain of paperwork that had turned up, he came across a letter from Rick Kirby. It informed Jack that he had been retained as a solicitor for Jack if needed, this just helped convince Ray that Kirby was deeper involved than he was letting on. It still didn't explain how he had turned up at the station so quickly after Jack had been brought in for questioning and Rays' thought on this was that whoever were the brains behind the operation obviously had people watching things all the time. Ray bagged all the papers up and marked them as evidence, then went back into the hallway.

'Right has anyone found anything else to interest us here?'

One Good Shot

'I don't think so Sir.' Replied the sergeant.

'Okay then, get this place sealed up and make your way back to the house and help the others there. I'm going to go back and see what else I can find out about this Kirby character.'

'Would that be Rick Kirby? Sir.'

'Yes why do you know him?'

'If it is the same guy I'm thinking of, I had dealings with him when I was stationed at Cambridge. He was a right smarmy guy even for a solicitor.'

This brought a smile to Rays' face,

'Right lad you come with me back to the station and see if it is the same guy. Also you might be able to give us some background to work with.'

'Okay Sir.'

On the way back Jimmy Davies explained to Ray that they had come across Kirby on a regular basis at Cambridge. He was the sort of solicitor who didn't seemed perturbed who he worked for or who paid his wages, as long as the money paid was a good amount. It was obvious that Kirby had realised early in his career that there was a lot of money to be made from keeping criminals out of jail. Jimmy also grudgingly admitted that Kirby was good at his job and that certain people in the underworld were willing to hire him. Ray listened to all this then said.

'Well hopefully this time he has slipped up and we can tie him into things as well. I will want to find out how he knew that French had been arrested really before some of us did.'

Back at the station Ray and Jimmy made their way to

the cells for Jimmy to identify Kirby. Jimmy looked through the window in the cell door and grinned.

'Yes that is him Sir.'

This made Ray feel better. It would mean that he had more bargaining power when interviewing either man. Just as quickly he also realised there was now a slight problem. This being that Kirby could no longer act as Jack Frenchs' solicitor while he was also being investigated. Ray asked Jimmy to stay around as he felt he could be of help in questioning Kirby. He asked Jimmy to go and dig through his own notes and anything else he could think of to give Ray as much background information as possible on Kirby. Ray always enjoyed seeing how enthusiastic officers got when given something to get their teeth into. Ray took the opportunity to make a quick call to Jenny. Unusually she was alone in the office when he rang so they were able to talk comfortably for a while without feeling that they were being watched or overheard. Ray told her what had been happening and that he hoped to be able to return home soon, it was if he could sense the smile on her face when he spoke this lifted his spirits and a silly grin broke out on his face. He really couldn't remember the last time he had feelings like this. Suddenly Jenny changed the conversation back to the case so Ray realised someone had entered the room. He said his goodbyes and hung up. His next task was to go and see the custody officer.

Chapter Eighteen

'You will need to speak to both Mr. Kirby and Mr. French. They are going to both need some new legal representation.'

The desk sergeant looked up,

'That is going to go down well with Mr. Kirby I can't imagine him being happy with a duty solicitor. I will get it arranged as soon as possible.'

'I would think that he most probably would have someone he would like to use. Jack French would take no notice who is sitting in with him.'

Ray made his way to see Robert to discuss how they were now going to progress with the investigation. Robert was pleased with how things were now going. After talking to Ray he felt the case was close to being wrapped up.

'How much do we know about this Kirby character?'

'Not a lot at the moment. But from what some of the others have told me, I have the feeling he is certainly involved in some way. And I think it is quite possible he has been helping the people behind this for some time.'

'Work on finding out from him what you can. It will also help us put pressure on French.'

'We are just now waiting on new solicitors to be

appointed. I agree with you that Kirby is the weak link and will respond to pressure, French is much calmer. That could have a lot to do with the fact that when you think about it he is a professional killer.'

Ray was hopeful that by finding out who had hired Rick Kirby and any other contacts he had. This would lead them to the people behind everything and the person who had ordered the killing of Joe. When Ray got back to the custody suite the sergeant told him that a solicitor for Mr. Kirby was waiting. Ray was not surprised at the speed that Rick had managed to arrange a solicitor, he understood that people of the same profession would be there for each other. He did wonder how the person involved would respond when he knew the full facts of why they wanted to speak to Mr. Kirby about. He also explained that they were having difficulty finding someone to represent Jack. He went on to explain that the two numbers Jack had given them for solicitors both had refused to come and see him.

'This suggests to me Sir that he has been left on his own by whoever. So I have contacted the duty solicitor who has told me he is busy but will get here as soon as possible.'

'We can make a start with Kirby then.'

In the interview room Ray turned on the tape machine and announced himself and D.S. Stephen Summer who had offered to help out with the interviews.

'Also present Mr. Rick Kirby and his solicitor.'

'I am Jonathon Quick. I wish it to be noted on record that I feel this is highly irregular.'

'Oh I think as we explain things it will all become clear. First I would like your client to tell me who hired him.'

'Mr. Kirby doesn't have to divulge that information.'

One Good Shot

'True I agree. But it would help us all and make this questioning easier.'

'I would just like to ask, what crime are you accusing my client of?'

'Well we can start with accessory to murder.'

Rick Kirby looked as though someone had put a pin in a balloon as all the air rushed out of his body. He slumped forward onto the table.

'How on earth can you suggest a respected solicitor is tied in with a murder?'

'It will be better for us all, if you stop trying to paint your client as some sort of angel. We already know he represents some of the shadier characters we deal with. Also he is not too bothered who pays his bills.'

'You can't hold it against him, for how he makes his living. Everyone deserves a fair chance.'

'Very commendable, tell that to Joe Kippers' widow. Even you can't believe he only does the work he does and who for, out of a conscience.'

Mr. Quick looked over at Rick and then spoke,

'I think that is enough of the bantering. Shall we get down to the real business, and then we can get this mess sorted out quickly.'

'That would seem like a good idea. Mr. Kirby can you tell us how you are involved with Jack French?'

'I have known Mr. French for several years. As you will be aware he has been harassed by the police in the past for many petty things. Also I think it needs recording that they have never had cause to charge Mr. French with anything, so it does appear that they just like harassing him.'

'I can assure you I'm not harassing him, I would just like

Ken Ward

to get the truth. Also you must realise we are not dealing with anything petty here. You already know that Mr. French is being held on a murder charge. We have also recovered the murder weapon at his home.'

Before any further conversation was possible, there was a knock at the door. D.S. Summer answered; he then gave Ray a note. This told Ray that the duty solicitor had arrived and was speaking to Jack French.

'I think that now we have put you in the picture as to how things are progressing, it would be a good idea to suspend this interview. You need to think about where you go from here. It is obvious to me that you are being used by some very nasty people, you are happy with this because you were well rewarded. Even you must realise that they are also willing to let you take the blame for the mess.'

Ray was not surprised to see a slightly worried look on Mr. Quick's face after he had finished speaking and he felt that this would help, as he hoped he would explain to Rick how by him helping the police it would in turn help him, when this mess was to come to court which it was obvious was the next phase of the proceedings.

Ray left the two of them in the room. He could see by his face that Rick was very quickly weighing up his options. Ray and Stephen walked along the corridor to see Jack and the duty solicitor. As they approached the door they heard raised voices. Ray held Stephen back from opening the door.

'Someone doesn't sound happy. Let's leave them for a bit and get coffee. If they have argued, it is possible that Jack will not be so alert. Also I think that something else needs looking at here. It may appear trivial, but I am amazed that if French has been spoken to before that he is not in the system. Surely fingerprints would have been taken.'

'All we can do about that Sir is ask someone to find out why, but depending on what he was questioned about and the circumstances. His details would not be the first persons to go missing would they?'

Ray realised this was true, but would make sure that everyone knew his feelings on the matter, once they had things tied up. Ray had always let it be known to people he worked with the importance of making sure everything was done properly. Especially with solicitors like Mr. Kirby about.

Stephen was glad for the break. This was his first direct involvement with a murder case. He was listening and learning as things progressed. Ray was not the sort to switch off, so while they drank their coffee he talked through the case with Stephen. Ray had always found he worked well by getting other peoples input in cases. He could sense that Stephen was willing to learn and he could see potential for him in the future.

'I think you are right in that Rick Kirby knows more than he is letting on to us.'

'Yes I think it is now a case of pushing the right buttons. Then he might be more helpful.'

'Do you think that he is thinking to himself that if he tells us too much, he could be causing more trouble for himself?'

'Probably, I think it is time to go and shake Mr. French up.'

The atmosphere in the interview room was distinctly

frosty. There was a deliberate gap between the chairs that Jack and his new solicitor were occupying.

'I am Mr Kennedy. I will be representing Mr. French. He has instructed me that I am only here as a precaution, he will answer your questions if he feels like it.'

Ray looked at the solicitor and could see that he wasn't impressed by things. Ray realised he would be billing the time he was sat here for. Being a duty solicitor Mr. Kennedy didn't have the luxury of being able to pick and chose his clients. He would usually be called in by the police to deal with drunks. Or other cases where people had no means of legal representation. He would have thought that a high profile case like this would do his career some good, being told by Jack that he didn't want his help would have been a blow. As soon as Ray had switched on the tapes and everyone had introduced themselves. Jack began to speak,

'Right we all know why I'm here, so let's see if I can clear things up for you quickly.'

Immediately Ray was wary. He saw no reason why Jack would say anything that was liable to help them. Jack continued,

'All I am willing to say is that yes, I was involved with the deaths of Joe Kipper and Ted Bloom. No I don't know who paid me. I'm prepared to face the consequences of my actions, but you will not get any help from me to deal with the matter further.'

Lee Kennedy sat open mouthed at this confession. He felt he really was out of his depth in the room. At the same time Ray and Stephen found it difficult to believe what they had just heard.

'That is a great help Mr. French. I'm sure the crown

prosecution service will be happy to take you to court on two counts of murder.'

'Whatever, I can behave myself and do some time. Then apply for parole.' Jack laughed as he spoke.

'Oh I'm not sure it will be as easy as you imagine. The one thing that most people who I work with know about me is I nearly always get the result I'm looking for. I can do this by being nice or I can be a right bastard. And I don't think parole is your option here.'

This speech took Jack by surprise.

'What do you mean by that then?'

'Well it is very commendable that you are prepared to take the fallout for this, and not involve anyone else. And once I put the word round in the right peoples ears, prison life might not be as easy as you think.'

Lee went to speak only to be cut off by Jack.

'And what can you say to anyone?'

'You would be surprised at the people who respect me, Mr. French. They might be inside but they still feel I helped them. I can just let certain people know how you helped us with our enquiries, and you would be amazed how many people get upset by such news.'

'You can't threaten me like that.'

'Just you watch me. And it is not a threat it is a promise. I will find out who is behind the murder of Joe Kipper.'

Stephen was taken aback by how Ray had changed his attitude. In particular since Jack had admitted the two murders. He felt most officers would have been satisfied with a conclusion like that. Ray appeared to be like a dog with a bone and he seemed to want more.

Jack now turned to his solicitor. Lee seemed to be amused now he appeared to be needed.

'How do I stand to complain about how I am being treated by this idiot?'

'If I was you I would watch how you refer to him. I don't see what I can advise you to do. You wouldn't listen to me in the first place. You have admitted the crimes; surely it would be better for you now to help the police. It could work in your favour.'

'Not when I think about it. I was hired to deal with people who didn't do as asked. So you don't need to be a genius to work out what would happen to me.'

Lee looked at Jack then turned his attention to Ray.

'Is there anything you can offer my client, if you get the information you require?'

'It is not going to be easy. He is facing two murder charges. It could help him if any information he gave us helped get the main people behind all this. How about I arrange for some coffee to be brought in and leave you to discuss it between yourselves.'

Chapter Nineteen

Ray and Stephen left the room. There was a stunned silence behind them. Jack was seriously thinking about Rays' last few comments. Lee Kennedy was feeling that he wished someone else had been duty solicitor today.

'Stephen if you go and let the team know what has happened. I will go and see the superintendant and also ring my station to bring them up to date.'

Robert was impressed how things had moved on. He also agreed that it would be good if they could get to Jack to give them some help.

'So what is your next move then?'

'Well I think he can help us. Though I feel he may be telling the truth about knowing very little about who pays him. The other stumbling point could be that I'm very loath to suggest doing any sort of deal with him.'

'You can only speak to him and let him know initially that you will put in a word with the C.P.S to let them know he was cooperative. He must realise it is not like the films with special deals being made. Also you need to explain to him that making deals is not down to us, any help given to him would depend on the results of help he gives us. Even then it would be for the hierarchy to decide on any deal. If he could just give us a name it could flag up something that is maybe already being looked at in the betting scams. From what information you have given me it is big business so we should have something on record.'

'It is a possibility. I will ring Adam, then go back and see if Mr. French has had any more thoughts. Slight change of subject Robert but Stephen Summer seems to be a very good officer.'

'I know I think he has a good career ahead of him. I like to think I have helped some of my officers with their future. I might be more of a pen pusher now but I do remember what being on the streets was like.'

Ray smiled as he left he wished that Adam would remember that sometimes instead of just wanting forms all filled in correctly so it looked good to his superiors. When Ray was on the phone he couldn't help but feel cautious. Adam was obviously pleased that they now had a result on the shooting. He felt this was look good for the local force. Ray would just like to get more details on the betting scam and the crooks behind it all.

'I know that French pulled the trigger. The people who paid for it are really the ones who killed Joe and Ted.'

'You just have to accept that Jack French may well be all you can get from this.'

'We will see. The brief Rick Kirby could be the key to more. He is extremely nervous about things. If we can get to look at his paperwork, and find out who is retaining him it could open everything up for us.'

'You surely know what I'm going to say next Ray.'

Ray took a deep breath this was the bit he didn't want to hear.

One Good Shot

'Be careful how much time you spend on this. You have got the killer. Don't get carried away and be satisfied with a good result.'

'How can I be satisfied? When I know this goes a lot deeper, it is very likely that more people have been killed by this organization. It may be a cliché but they are like a cancer, it is not always obvious that it is there and sometimes once it is spotted it spreads quickly. I just want to get to the root of the problem and stamp out as much as it is possible to do. They target people who are vulnerable then when needed they exact a nasty revenge. So why should I and all the others who have put time and sweat into this case leave it halfway finished, just to please some pen pusher at head office who wants to show we haven't spent too much money.'

Ray felt better after this speech and Adam was obviously taken aback by his passion. He liked Ray as an officer but was always determined to make sure his superiors could see what a good job he did in controlling the purse strings.

'Okay Ray. Spend some time on it but just remember what I've said. There is plenty here that also needs your attention.'

This seemed to be permission to carry on and also a rebuke all in one go.

'I can't see there is anything more pressing than a murder enquiry. But I accept what you are saying Sir. I will speak to Tim as he has already dealt with the betting scam. He can follow it up in more depth now.'

Ray got transferred to Tim in the incident room.

'Tim I want you to go back over the details behind the

betting. Look out for any mention of the names of Jack French and also another name for you is Rick Kirby.'

'I will get on with it now, apart from the names anything else to help.'

'Sorry at the moment no. But if you can find out who has been paying Kirby it could be a big help.'

'It would help if I could see some of his paperwork Sir.'

'I have already arranged for someone to get that organized. He is only a one man band operation, and usefully he is known to some of the local officers. There is an application for a warrant in process to allow us into his office; we will see what that turns up. As soon as they find any paperwork I will see that it is faxed to you.'

Ray made his way to continue the interview with Jack French. He saw Stephen in the canteen, who came over to join him.

'Stephen, my boss has given me some time to concentrate on the betting scam. I know that it is the background to all this case, it is just a case of getting some evidence.'

'So how do we progress with this?'

'Hopefully French is sensible enough to accept the help we can offer, if he helps us. He must know something about his paymaster.'

Stephen knew that this could now be the hardest piece of the case. He realised they had got this far after some lucky breaks as well as good detective work. It was obvious that Jack was only interested in protecting himself. It had caught him unawares when Ray had threatened Jack; he was willing to accept that the method worked if Jack now came up with some names.

One Good Shot

The first thing they noticed when they entered the room, was how deflated Jack now looked compared to when they had first spoken to him.

'So have you had time to think? Where we go from here is now down to you.'

'Before I even think of giving you any information. I need to know that you will protect me. These people can reach everywhere.'

'You are going to have to give me some important information first. Then it will be decided what help you can have. We don't do deals lightly; also you need to remember you are here because you killed two people that we know about.'

'I have got to know I will be looked after. Anything I tell you could get me killed.'

'Sounds very dramatic. Just a bit over the top. Do you agree Stephen?'

Stephen reacted quickly to being brought into the conversation. This impressed Ray.

'I think he is trying to make it sound important, mainly for our benefit Sir.'

'I agree. Come on Jack at least start by giving us a name that we can work with.'

'All I will say at the moment is trying looking into a thug called Pete. I only know his first name; he goes by the nickname of Steel Man. I have never had dealings with him before and it makes me nervous when I don't know someone.'

Stephen left the room to get it moving for checking the names. Jack continued talking as though nothing had happened.

'I always work alone that is better for me. Then this time they involved this thug to try and scare Ted Bloom. I was just instructed to take him out as they didn't feel the warning had worked.'

'We will see if this person exists, then see where we go next.'

'I know he exists. Just remember I need assurances before I say anymore.'

Stephen had come back into the room. It was fortunate that the Steel Man was known to the local boys. His full name was Pete Hughes. His history was he was a local thug who for the right money would do most things.'

Ray wound up the interview by telling Jack he needed more from him. He arranged with Mr. Kennedy to return to the station in two hours to see how things were progressing. Jack was returned to his cell.

'Stephen I want you to get things moving to pick up this Hughes as soon as possible. Someone pays him and if he is just hired muscle he may be inclined to speak to us to save him grief.'

Once Ray was alone he made his way to the canteen, and found himself a quiet corner. He closed his eyes and took a deep breath. He had always had good self control of his emotions while working cases. Maybe this had come with age he really wasn't sure, for some reason this case was pushing that control to the limit. He could only put it down to the fact that several people including Adam were telling him that having someone in custody for two murders should be satisfying. Ray just couldn't shake the feeling that he was letting people down and letting others away with things, if he didn't find out who was behind everything.

Chapter Twenty

Ray left the canteen having decided in his own mind the next course of action. He knew he had to deal with things and not allow personal feelings to get in the way. If he was to look at things objectively he realised that he had to be happy, with the results that had been achieved in the case. He was also coming to terms with how he felt about Jenny and in as much as he knew there could be problems ahead; he wasn't prepared to let the job get in the way. When his wife died he had felt that all he had left was work. And he threw himself headlong into it, any extra that needed doing he was always there as he explained to all the others he had nothing waiting at home for him. He didn't realise at first but slowly it registered that Jenny was spending more time volunteering to help out when things needed clearing up. She had started off by being someone he could talk to then they went for a drink after work and things went from there. He was always the pessimist and trying to keep things calm. Jenny was more up front about things and would constantly offer ideas such as her getting transferred. In as much as this wasn't what he wanted he was now coming around to the idea as long as they could then get on with their lives. Rays' thoughts were as long as the job was done properly there was no reason they couldn't be together. He pushed these thoughts to one side as he went to see Robert to explain how he felt they should now tie things up.

Ray entered the office just as Robert was finishing on the phone.

'Good news for you Ray.'

'I feel like I could do with some.'

'They have found phone records and money transfers, to both this thug Pete Hughes and the solicitor Kirby. They are both receiving payments from someone called Jun Sheng.'

'Well that does sound like the sort of name that they would mix with. I don't think so. So do we presume he could be the link to the betting scam?'

'I would say it is a distinct possibility. Some of the lads brought Hughes in about ten minutes ago, so you are now in the position to ask them both about it.'

'I will get round to talking to them. First I think we should get Jack French processed. We can charge him with the murders of Bloom and Joe Kipper.'

'You sound about down about it Ray, surely it is a good result?'

'Yes it is. I know that French isn't going to be able to give us any more information, but I just feel these guys behind the scam should be held more responsible. As far as Adam is concerned we have our killer and I should be satisfied. I just have a feeling that these other people are behind maybe so many more killings.'

'I understand your feelings. We have to work with the evidence, we have our killer and I would agree with leaving it there. But now with this name it could be worth carrying

One Good Shot

on for a bit, and we can get the name Jun Sheng circulated to see what comes forward.'

Ray brightened up at the fact he felt he was getting some support from Robert.

'I will ring and speak to Adam. I know we are all being followed by the finance people, but if we can tie these people into things we are surely just doing our job properly.'

'That would be really helpful; I know Adam is always under pressure about costs. It doesn't help that we are classed as a small country station. Our area is just as big as some of the other areas but we are more spread out. The big thing at the moment is all about mergers with other forces. The people upstairs just don't seem to know what it is like out on the streets.'

'I understand all that you are saying. Just leave that side of things to me and you go and get French sorted and make sure it is all watertight so there are no problems when it comes to court.'

'That won't happen. Even though it will not make a lot of difference in court we need to let the prosecution know that he did help with some information.'

Ray left as Robert was ringing Lynn to speak with Adam, there was now a spring back in his step as he felt he now had more support to get as many as possible of the people involved. Before he went to the custody suite he went outside and did something he had never done before. He rang Jenny on her mobile at work. He could tell as she answered she was surprised.

'Hello you.'

Jenny could hear the smile in his voice.

'This is nice to what do I owe the honour?'

Ken Ward

'I just wanted to let you know, I love you and that I think we should talk as soon as I can get back there. It may be awhile as the case has now moved on and I think we could get the money men who organized it all.'

'That is great news on both counts. Due to who is listening you will have to just take my answer as being I feel the same.'

If anyone could see a split picture of them both, they would see them both grinning as though they had both just won the lottery.

'I have got to go and start things moving again. I don't know when I will be back but it will be as quickly as I can make it happen.'

They finished their conversation and Ray went back in as Stephen came along the corridor. Ray explained what had happened over the last thirty minutes and was happy with Stephens' response.

'I hope that you feel I can still help out with the interviews and don't feel that you should bring in a more experienced officer Sir?'

'The thought had not crossed my mind. You have shown yourself perfectly capable so far, so lets' go and get things moving again.'

They started with the easy part now which was arranging that Jack French would make an appearance at Lynn Magistrates court as an initial move. Then it was most likely his case would be allocated a date at crown court and his murder trial would take place. It wouldn't be a long case unless he did anything like changing his plea. Ray felt this unlikely as Jack was shaken by the things Ray had said in the interview; also he was the sort of person who knew he had to face the consequences of his actions.

Ray finished with custody sergeant by organizing solicitors for both Mr. Hughes and Mr. Kirby so that they could start the questioning of them both. Phone calls had already been made Mr. Quick would continue to represent Kirby and the duty solicitor was on his way back one to see what had happened with Jack French and he would be the legal team for Hughes. Ray was again feeling happier about the case and this time he didn't think anything could happen to spoil this. He would do what was necessary to prove he was right to want to continue with things.

Before Ray could continue with the interviews, he was handed some paperwork by another officer. It transpired that on initial checks they had been rewarded with the name Jun Sheng coming up as having been investigated by fraud officers previously. There was not a lot to go on as it was noted that the investigating officers had just placed his name on the system so that if anyone else was to look into things involving him it would be flagged up. This would then give officers something to look into which may help their own investigation. It also meant that forces around the country and now the globe would not waste time with the possibility of more than one team just following another's work. Ray knew this would be of help when he spoke to both Kirby and Hughes.

Chapter Twenty One

Ray knew that this was now going to be the hardest part of the case. He had the killer and some of the others involved, it was unfortunate that Ted Bloom had been killed. And though Ray knew it was part of his job to see the people responsible convicted, he couldn't help but feel the main people to care for in this case were Joe and Alison. If Ted had been more forthcoming maybe he would still be alive. Being honest with himself, all he could hope to gain from the upcoming interviews was to glean enough information to then pass onto the international teams of officers around the world, who had dealings with this type of crime. It had become clear that the F.A. had been doing what they could to stamp out the problem. The problem of betting scams in sport was spread worldwide and it always had been that if you gave a person the chance of winning some money by betting on their favourite in sport, there were others who would try and make more money out of it.

He turned to Stephen and spoke,

'I think we will start with Mr. Kirby. Even though he is obviously a good solicitor I think he could be the weaker of the two people we have to talk with.'

They entered the interview room and Rick Kirby was

One Good Shot

visibly shaken by the events he was now part of. Jonathan Quick was sitting more comfortably beside his client they both looked resigned to the fact that Rick telling the truth as he knew it to be was the best course of action. Ray had only just finished all the preliminaries with the tape machine when Rick started talking.

'I know I am in trouble because of how I have helped these people out. I'm not sure what you are going to charge me with but I would like to say on record I never knew anyone was going to be killed.'

'If you just start at the beginning for us please Mr. Kirby and explain how you were contacted and who this Jun Sheng is.'

'Jun Sheng was the person who made contact with me. I like a bet and a drink as do a lot of people. I have never got in out of my depth, but I was a regular in Ted Blooms' shop. One day after I had placed a few bets, I got a phone call at the office from Mr. Sheng who explained he worked for a group of foreign business men who liked to gamble. They wanted someone in this country to help them with their accounts and also to act as a solicitor for some of their people if needed.' Rick paused and took a deep breath as though he was building himself up to keep talking. "Being a solicitor working on my own I was not adverse to doing extra work if it was going to pay well and from what I was told this was certainly going to do that."

Ray didn't want to stop Rick from talking but felt they needed to keep things on track of where the investigation was going.

'So how much work have you done for these people?'

'I have had a look at their books. This is mainly a cover

up for any betting they have arranged in this country and keeps things smooth with the authorities. Mainly it seemed that Ted Bloom was the main bookmaker they used in this country, but it is possible he had given them other names of people to work with. I have represented a couple of people for them on minor offences. I think it has been the main aim to keep them out of prison and make sure there were no awkward questions asked, to lead officers to investigate further.'

Jonathan Quick now felt it right to speak up.

'I think my client has been more than helpful in your enquiries and I would hope you would look favourably on this?'

'It seems people keep asking me to do them favours today just because they give me information. If these people had not broken the law in the first place we wouldn't have this situation. All I will say is that I'm grateful for the help Mr. Kirby is now giving us and I'm sure the C.P.S. will take it into consideration. But be aware I will do all I can to make sure that your client never works as a solicitor again, it makes my blood boil to think how he has helped these men and it has led to needless deaths.'

Ray finished the interview by charging Rick with perverting the course of justice and having him taken back to the cells.

'Right Stephen it is time for us to see what this Hughes character has to say for himself.'

'Okay Sir, ready when you are.'

'Tell you what, how do you feel about leading the questioning this time?'

Stephen felt himself fill up with pride even though he

One Good Shot

felt it wasn't the correct way to respond he couldn't help himself.

'You don't have to look so chuffed with yourself. You have earnt the chance I think.'

They went along to the room where they had been told Mr. Hughes was waiting along with Lee Kennedy the duty solicitor. Lee was looking more comfortable this time as he felt his client would let him do his job.

Stephen switched the tape on and all present introduced themselves.

'Mr. Hughes I would like to start by asking you what you know about a person called Jun Sheng?'

'Don't know who you are on about son.'

'Well if you are saying you don't know him that is strange. He has been paying you money for some time; I presume it is not just a gift now and then.'

Pete looked over at Lee who raised his eyebrows and said.

'I would say that having seen this gentlemen work today if they have a name, then they already have some idea of what your answers should be. It could be of help to you if you tell them what they want to know.'

Ray sighed, 'Here we go again more favours being asked of the nice policemen.'

This attitude shook Pete and he looked to Lee for more help. He had been in trouble in the past but usually it had just been for fighting, and he had never been to prison. With his sentences from the courts normally being bound over to keep the peace or thanks to the work Rick Kirby had done he had escaped with just a caution he felt that this time was

Ken Ward

entirely different and he was becoming more concerned as to where this would lead.

'Just answer them; it really would be for the best.'

'Okay. Ted told me I could earn some extra money by being around when these people who Sheng represented needed someone reminding of their obligations. I have always been handy with the muscle so it seemed okay to me if someone just needed a nudge in the right direction.'

Stephen looked over at Ray and said.

'Well this time you giving them a nudge didn't work and consequently two people are dead. I think we may as well leave the interview there. You will be charged with threatening behaviour towards people and also we will oppose any application for bail that you may make when this goes to court as it is considered that you would try to avoid any further court appearances. So you may as well be where we know you are. I'm sure by the time the investigation is finished there may be more charges.'

Pete was taken away and Ray looked at Stephen.

'Well done you handled that well.'

'Thanks Sir. If I'm honest I think I just need a coffee now. Do you think they might be able to charge him with more as at the moment I think he is getting away lightly. I think he has possibly been involved in more than just giving people a frightening warning.'

'Go on then you have earnt it. And just to put your mind at rest I agree with your thoughts, I will make sure that they look hard into the dealings Hughes had with everything so we get him on what we can. Enjoy your coffee but don't forget you will need to now type up your report to go with the rest of the mountain of paperwork there is already.'

One Good Shot

Ray sat quietly in the room he realised that there was nothing else he could do on the case. It was now down to others to carry on the work that he and his team had started. He was feeling happier with this outcome to the case and went to see Robert. Then he knew he would be able to head back home, and start sorting things out with Jenny. As he thought of her he couldn't stop himself from smiling, this feeling convinced that he had to now follow his heart. It was as if he had made several decisions all at once, and he knew that happiness was something that may not come along very often and with the things he saw in the job, he had to take every chance. He even felt that he could deal with any problems raised by his superiors about the relationship just knowing that Jenny wanted the same things out of life.

Chapter Twenty Two

Ray left the interview room. His next job was to make sure everything was tidied up with Robert before he left. Robert was quite happy that Jack French was being dealt with by the courts in Lynn, his force still had the others and it would look good to the authorities once the betting scam had been investigated further. They both agreed that it wasn't the best way of things being run but clear up figures were all that seemed to matter these days. Robert stood and shook hands as he said,

'So you will be making your way back to Lynn now then?'

'Yes I better get back and see what else has been happening while I've been here. I'm sure there will be plenty of work on my desk, even though it will appear to be mundane after this past case.'

After having said his goodbyes, he made the journey home. There was always a slight empty feeling once a case had been wrapped up. Ray knew it wouldn't be long before there would be something else that would need his attention. When he got back to Lynn his first job was to contact Alison, she was still at her parents holiday home in Blakeney and as much as Ray would have liked a trip to the coast he

One Good Shot

knew he would have a pile of paperwork to do so he made do with letting her know what had happened over the phone. He explained all that had happened and that the person who had killed Joe was now under arrest. This at least allowed her closure on that part of things. He could tell by her voice and attitude, that slowly she would be able to rebuild some sort of life. Ray finished the call by wishing her the best for the future even though he knew it would be difficult. He also told her if she felt she needed to discuss anything else to do with the events of the past few weeks she could just ring. Alison thanked him for this and all the work the team had done to help her.

The following morning Ray walked through the doors of the station and was greeted by hellos', then a pile of paperwork that seemed precariously balanced on his desk. He knew his next couple of days would be spent going through this work as well as making sure all paperwork on the case was up to date. He also needed figures ready to show the finance people that everything that had been spent on the investigation was warranted. He was sitting signing off some of the easier papers when he felt the presence at his door. He looked up to see the smiling face of Jenny. Her smile grew even more as he returned the look,

'Do you know how good it is to see you back?'

'Very I would hope. The next question we have is what do we do next?'

'I know what I want to do, but that might have to wait till later.' She laughed in reply. "I suppose you already have some ideas as to what happens next?"

'Yes but I think we should meet tonight and discuss them together. Then we will tell who needs to know.'

'Right I shall see you later, are we meeting at the restaurant?'

'Yes that sounds good I will book the table for eight o'clock and meet you there.'

Ray knew he would now have to go and explain everything to Adam. He also felt that he may well have to apologise after his outburst on the phone. The one thing he hoped for was that Robert had already phoned and maybe down some of the work in his favour, by reporting how pleased he was with the outcome that had been achieved. As he knocked and went in he felt comfortable that Adam was content with things.

'I suppose congratulations are in order in that you got the result you wanted.'

'I would hope that it was the result we all would have hoped for Sir.'

'Well okay then, but I didn't appreciate the way you spoke to me on the phone nor that Robert has rung to tell me how well you did.'

'I apologise if you were offended Sir. I only spoke how I felt about things and I hope that the result does show I was right to a degree. I know we have our differences Sir, but I would hope that out of respect for each other we can see that the result is what matters.'

'Yes I know that and I know you are good at your job. But it is not you who has to show the top brass reasons for us spending money.'

'No, I agree but all the paperwork is up to date and it shows that the spending was merited. If the investigation carries on as well as it has so far into the betting scams, then

One Good Shot

everyone should be happy that the job was worth it. After all surely that is what we are here for?'

'Okay then just make sure I have all I need, on my desk by this afternoon. I have a meeting soon and will tell the others how well we did in clearing the case up. It should help when they discuss merging forces that we are able to show what the team is capable of.'

Ray left the office with a smirk on his face. It was a surprise how that now they had got a conviction with possibly others to follow that Adam was happy to say how well the station had worked on things. This was the one area of the job that always annoyed Ray he had spent his working days on the force always doing the hard work and though he would praise his team for their work, he didn't like it how the top ranks would try to take the praise but always passed things down the ranks when it was a problem to be sorted or bad news. The rest of the day passed quietly enough and he made his way to the restaurant feeling contented with things and he was hopeful that if Jenny agreed with him then by the end of the evening things in his personal life were going to be better as well.

Jenny was already sitting at the table when he walked in. He stood and admired her first without her knowing he was there. As she turned and smiled he just felt so good. They sat and ordered then Jenny spoke first,

'Come on then what is your big idea for us?'

'Well if it is okay with you, I would like to suggest that you put in to transfer to Tallenbee as I think you would do well there. I know it means you being the one to move for work, but it would be easier for you to transfer than me. Also it is possible you could put in for a promotion to tie in

Ken Ward

with it all. Then there is nothing to stop us seeing each other without the secrecy.'

Ray waited expectantly for her response and he could feel his heart starting to slow as he held his breath. Slowly the smile was there again as Jenny reached for his hand across the table.

'Sounds like a good idea, but do you think I would get the transfer?'

'If I speak to the right people there is no reason why not. That is one privilege of rank and also knowing who to speak too.'

The rest of the evening passed in a blur as they both had their own thoughts about the future. Ray even suggested that they could look for a house more central for them both. Until he had spoken to Adam they ended this evening as they usually did by going their separate ways in their own cars. But there was a different atmosphere in both cars as they pulled out onto the main road.

Ray decided to call back into the station on his way home just to check that all was now returning to normal after the enquiry. He walked through the corridors and saw that the incident room had been cleared away. All the officers would now return to the day to day work of policing. Tim Jarvis would be spending the next few days in contact with other officers bringing them up to date on what he had found out about all the betting that was going on. Ray would oversee the team in their work.

As he went to go home he was met by the duty sergeant.

'Nice to see you back Sir.'

One Good Shot

'Thanks though from your face I feel there is not good news.'

'Sorry but I think this is for you. Two lads have just phoned through they have found the body of a youngster in the park. It is lying underneath Greys Tower.'

Ray looked upwards and sighed as usual the job had a way of soon pulling you back to reality.

'Okay get a crew over there and tell them I'm on my way.'

As Ray spoke he got a horrible feeling in the pit of his stomach. He knew he would have to wait till he saw the crime scene but from the amount he had just been told he had a nervous flashback to a case he worked on when he first came to the C.I.D. in Lynn fifteen years ago. This had involved children being killed then laid out as though in sacrifice and always around religious landmarks in the area. He really hoped this was going to be different.